I0573652

A VERY HERO NEW YEAR

MORE BOOKS BY SUZAN HARDEN
(Each series is in suggested reading order)

Bloodlines
Blood Magick
Zombie Love
Zombie Confidential
Zombie Wedding
Amish, Vamps & Thieves
Blood Sacrifice
Love, War & a Bulldog
Zombie Goddess
Ravaged
Sacrificed
Reality Bites
Ghouls in the Grocery Store
Resurrected
Bloodlines Shorts Anthology
Bloodlines: The First Boxed Set

Seasons of Magick
Spring
Summer
Autumn
Winter
The Seasons of Magick Anthology

Justice
Sword and Sorceress 28 ("Justice")
Sword and Sorceress 30 ("Diplomacy in the Dark")
Justice: The Beginning
A Question of Balance
A Modicum of Truth
A Matter of Death
A Touch of Mother
A Twist of Love
A Virtue of Child
A Hand of Father
A Measure of Knowledge
A Hint of Thief

The Justice Thalia Stories
Snowfall
Murder Most Fowl
The Sweetest Poison
A Granddaughter of Mine

Tales of the Twelve
The Trickster Priestess and the Demon

888-555-HERO
Hero De Facto
Hero Ad Hoc
Hero De Novo
A Very Hero Christmas
Hero De Jure
Hero In Camera
Hero Amicus Curiae
A Very Hero Wedding
A Very Hero New Year
Hero Ad Litem
Queer Eye for the Super Guy

Solar System Services, Inc.
Alone Is Not Lonely

Millersburg Magick Mysteries
Spells and Sleuths
Fae and Felonies
Magick and Murder

Soccer Moms of the Apocalypse
Pestilence in Pumpkin Spice
Famine In French Vanilla
War in White Chocolate
Death in Double Mocha

Miscellaneous
Sword and Sorceress 31 ("Pig-Headed")
Sword and Sorceress 32 ("Unexpected")
Practical Witches
Revenge Served Hot
The Yule Switch
Chocolate for Dinner
Silver Shoes and Pigs' Ears

For updates, news, and giveaways, join Suzan's mailing list or visit her website at www.suzanharden.com. You can also check her out on Twitter or Facebook.

This is a work of fiction. All characters, organizations and events in this story are products of the author's imagination and are not to be construed as real. Any resemblance to persons, living or dead, is entirely coincidental.

A VERY HERO NEW YEAR (888-555-HERO #9)
Copyright 2022 by Suzan Harden
All rights reserved
ISBN-13: 978-1-64918-021-6

Published by Angry Sheep Publishing
Findlay, Ohio

Interior Design by JW Manus
Cover Design by For the Muse Designs

A Very Hero New Year

888-555-HERO #9

SUZAN HARDEN

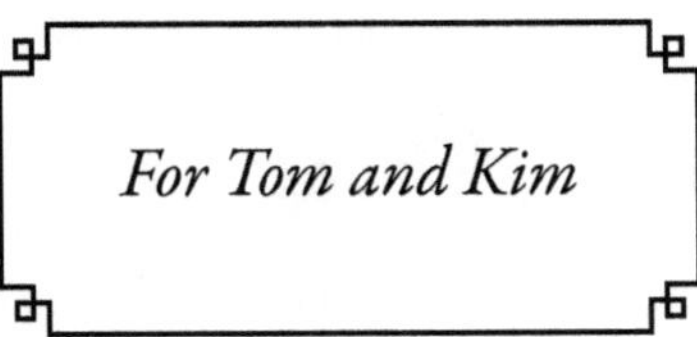

For Tom and Kim

CHAPTER 1

The party sounds got louder as Steve Connors jogged at a normal human speed up the southeast stairwell of the Canyon Pointe University Law School building. When he pushed open the steel door to the rooftop patio, the music and laughter ratcheted up several decibels. The December post-finals party was in full swing.

The dry wind off the western desert kept the traffic fumes at street level. That left the odor of alcohol and intoxicated humans at the top of the seven-story edifice to mix with the sage and creosote-scented breeze.

Bethany Spears from his Con law class waved, and he strode over to the study group who'd become his friends. Carter Swift slapped him on the shoulder and shoved a cup of beer into Steve's hand. "It's about time Mr. A-plus showed up." Carter looked around him. "Now where's the hottie you claim you're dating?"

"She took her son to her parents' place for dinner tonight, and you can keep the cup." Steve pressed the red plastic back into his friend's hand. Carter's breath was enough to get everyone on the roof plastered.

Steve was more than a little disappointed Qiang refused to come. She claimed she got all her partying out of her system when she was an undergrad. The truth was situations like this underscored their age difference, and it made Qiang damn uncomfortable. Part of him understood. The rest of him tried to convince her no one would know her age unless she announced it.

For some reason, she didn't take that as the compliment he meant it to be.

Maybe, his perspective was skewed. People had always assumed he was older because of his size.

"I don't think this woman exists," Bethany remarked. "Unless Qiang is the nickname for your right hand."

"Oh, come on," Nick Lyons drawled. "For all you know, he could have bought one of those lifelike Japanese sex dolls."

Carter and Bethany roared with laughter.

Maybe it was a good thing Qiang didn't come after all. She would have electrocuted Nick's balls for saying that.

"Ha, ha." Steve rolled his eyes. "Thank you for proving her point she didn't want to spend a boring evening with a bunch of immature trust-fund babies."

"Hey, I resemble that remark." Carter waved his cup, sloshing beer over the side. "Maybe your mystery woman is really waiting for a rich and charming guy to sweep her off her feet."

"More like Prince Charming to sweep her floor," Nick shot back.

Steve snorted, and Bethany laughed out loud.

"I think I'll find something to drink before Carter washes the floor with all the beer." Steve headed for the corner where tables were set up with food, alcohol, and soft drinks.

He selected a plastic bottle of cola. The last thing he needed was to get drunk and accidentally display his powers. Though honestly, it would take every bit of beer and wine on the table to produce a slight buzz thanks to his metabolism.

For the last twelve years of his life, he'd been so careful to keep his secret, only to discover he had a twin with the exact same powers. A twin brother who was a noted and popular superhero.

A brother who despised him.

Steve stepped away from the crowd. The old guilt resurfaced though everyone told him Professor Paranoia kidnapping and controlling him wasn't his fault. Even Tim Canyon, AKA the original Ghost Owl, didn't blame Steve for the severe injuries he inflicted on the non-super. Tim was damn lucky he could walk again after what Steve had done. In fact, Tim insisted on training Steve in some basic self-defense techniques. Sparring with his brother Rey though often left him bruised despite his abilities.

Tim's lessons remained at the forefront of Steve's mind despite the festive atmosphere. He scanned the area. Red, green, and white lights lit up several buildings in downtown. A few other offices twinkled blue and white. Above all of them, the Del Oro Bank's red and gold eagle ruled the skyline.

A girl wearing a hoodie and jeans leaned against the retaining wall on the other side of the law school's roof. She wasn't staring at the lights of downtown. No, her head stretched over the edge of the ledge. A few of her braids waved in the breeze. There wouldn't be anything on that side of the building but the street, traffic, and pedestrians. The school didn't even have a door to enter on that side, so she couldn't be watching for someone who said they'd be here tonight.

Steve went back to the refreshment tables and grabbed a second bottle of cola. Before he strode halfway across the roof, the girl straightened and flung her right leg over the safety wall.

He raced toward her as fast as he could without using superspeed. "Hey—" Thankfully, she turned to look at him. Mariah Pendleton. She had been in several of his first year classes. Quiet, but she had the right answer every time one of the professors called on her.

"It's Mariah, right?" Steve said.

"Yeah." She looked at him suspiciously while she straddled the wall. A couple of her braids stuck out from beneath the hood of her sweatshirt. "Why aren't you with your friends, Connors?" A strong whiff of alcohol came from her.

"I went to get a drink, and I saw you over here by yourself." He held out one of the bottles of cola. "So I brought you one."

She shook her head. "Don't want it."

"I can get you orange? Root beer? Lemon-lime?"

"I don't want anything from you. Go away." Mariah looked down again and swung her other leg over the wall.

"Hey, that's kind of dangerous." Blood roared in his ears. Logic and debate he could handle. A drunk, distraught person planning to harm herself was way out of his wheelhouse.

"That's me. Stupid Mariah." A sob caught in her throat.

Steve looked back at the party. No one noticed what was going on over here, and he needed help. If he left to grab Bethany, Mariah would fall.

Or worse, jump.

He looked at Mariah who was studiously ignoring him in favor of the pavement. "You're not stupid, Mariah. You always know the answers when you're called on."

"Then why am I at the bottom of the class?" she wailed.

"We can all get the same exact score, and the profs still rank us," he said. "It's part of the stupidity of law school. We have to figure out what really matters."

"All that matters to my family is that I be the best." Mariah cried in earnest now. "I'm not. I can't go home."

Her pain infiltrated the scars of his heart. He understood. It didn't matter how much his adoptive parents loved him. He'd wondered his entire life why he wasn't good enough for his biological parents.

"Have you told them about your rank?" he asked.

"No." She hiccupped.

"Why does your rank matter more to your parents than whether you're learning the material?"

"Because they need to see the measurement." She gulped. "Because they told me if I wasn't in the top five percent, there was no reason to pay for my tuition."

"Wow," he muttered. "What a pair of douches."

"B-but they're right. I-I don't deserve the education if I can't do it."

"If money's an issue, I know a scholarship you could apply for." Steve edged over to the retaining wall and leaned against it. He peeked over the side. Yep, all concrete below. With her shaking and the amount of alcohol she had probably consumed, he needed to get her back on this side of the wall. "Why don't you come with me, and I can get the info for you?" He held out his free hand.

"Don't touch me!" she screeched.

"I won't if you climb back on this side of the wall," he assured her.

"Why would you care?" She finally looked at him. "Mister Top-of-the-Class," she spat.

"Maybe that's the difference," he said. "My parents don't really care about class rank. I don't have the same pressure on me that you do."

"Except you already have an internship with a firm," she said morosely.

Was that the real issue? She was jealous of him?

"Where did you hear that?" he asked.

"People talk." Mariah stared at the traffic below again.

"You do realize I'm working for my sister-in-law to pay for my room and board while I'm going to school, right?" he said dryly.

Mariah looked at him and sniffed. "You do realize that's still experience, right?"

Steve chuckled. "More like my brother got lucky, and his wife takes pity on me. Not to mention, it's a very small firm. They could use some help. I could set up a meeting—"

"I don't need your pity," Mariah snapped.

"It's not pity," he said. "Like I said rank is bullshit. You're the smartest person in our class. And my boss Harri would be the first one to say, 'What do you call someone who scores 675 on the Mojave bar exam?'"

"What?"

"A lawyer," he answered.

A slight giggle escaped from Mariah.

"And if you don't believe me, believe Harri. The bar exam has nothing to do with your class rank," he added. "And how you perform in the real world doesn't have anything to do with either of those things."

"I still don't want to go home for break." Mariah stared at the traffic below once again. "I can't face them, and I don't have any place to go."

"What if I find you a place to stay over break?" Steve said gently. "Would you climb back over the wall?"

Mariah sniffed again. "Like where?"

"I was going to offer the spare bedroom at my apartment," he said. "But if that is too weird for you, there are some other ladies in the building who would let you stay with them for a few days until we can figure something out."

"Okay." Mariah wiped at her eyes with the sleeve of her hoodie.

Some idiot blasted an air horn behind him. Mariah jerked. Her one hand on the retaining wall slipped from the concrete. In slow motion horror, he watched her drop.

Steve tossed aside the cola bottles, leapt over the retaining wall, and dived for the screaming Mariah.

CHAPTER 2

Still in her suit, Harri Winters flopped on her mattress, bouncing her fiancé Tim Canyon as he read on his tablet. Despite the cleaning she'd done to their loft last weekend, the entire place was still tainted with hints of sage, onions, and pumpkin spice.

Or maybe the last one was the cinnamon and vanilla-scented bath products their building manager's sons had gifted her for her birthday.

Tim looked at her over his reading glasses. "How did the interview go?"

"Urgh, argh."

"That good, huh?" He snickered.

"Steve and Patty cannot get licensed fast enough," she muttered.

"So what was the problem with this prospective associate?"

"Other than mansplaining superhero law to three of the attorneys who helped write the book on it?" She groaned. "I wasn't sure if Susan was going to tase him or Aisha would punch him through the wall."

"Have you had any problems with Travis?" Tim asked.

"Surprisingly, no." She rolled over on her side and propped her cheek on her fist. "Even Aisha admits he knows his stuff. We haven't had any issues with him not doing his work or the actual quality of his products. Plus, he's been very careful to walk the fine line between being too deferential and acting like a know-it-all."

Neither of Harri's partners had been happy when she first suggested bringing Travis Beckham on board as an associate. Aisha more so than Susan because Travis had been promoted over her at Dewey and Cheatham, their previous employer. Between Travis busting his ass to prove himself and a couple of former colleagues confirming Travis's story about him protecting his paralegal and secretary from the predatory excesses of the Dewey and Cheatham senior partners, Aisha's attitude had lightened up quite a bit.

"Were there any other former Dewey and Cheatham associates of the same caliber as Travis?" Tim asked.

"By the time the bankruptcy trustee laid off the remaining junior attorneys, there weren't that many left." She rolled onto her back and stared at the exposed beams of the loft. "Any quality ones resigned and either got a job or got the hell out of the state once Howard was arrested."

"What about someone you knew in law school like Susan?" Tim asked.

"They all want a bigger piece of the pie than we're willing to give them, or they're too scared of the targets we all have on our backs." She kicked off the sensible heels she'd worn to the interview dinner. They landed on the area rug with soft *thunks*. "It didn't help when we declined to represent Captain Mojave."

"I don't know." Tim chuckled. "Sourpuss seems to be having a great time on the talk show circuit, dishing about how he abandoned her and her sister after he knocked up their mother."

"Don't say that in front of Aisha," Harri chided. "None of this revenge tour is sitting well with her."

"Really? Wasn't she and Jeremy the ones who destroyed Quantum Commander's reputation?" Tim cocked his head. "How is that different than Captain Mojave getting punished for running around bad-mouthing the firm?"

"Quantum Commander's children weren't our clients," Harri said.

"Kerry's petty revenge stunt has nothing to do with needing an extra attorney," Tim pointed out.

"Unfortunately, we still have the same original problem," Harri said. "More billable work than four attorneys can reasonably do. Especially since the introduction campaign for Eagle Rising is about to start. Not to mention Aisha leaving in a month."

Despite Aisha laying out everything Harri would need to do for Paul Inunza's debut as a superhero, she still wished her best friend would stay in the U.S. long enough to hold her hand. The last thing Harri wanted to do was ruin the kid's chances of being a positive influence in the city. Especially with his mom currently in prison and his dad losing his job.

"Are you planning to go apeshit on me when she and Rey head to France?" Tim asked.

"Yep, but I'm limiting myself to one day of crying, gnashing my teeth, and rending my clothes." She grinned up at him. "Then I expect you to keep the freezer full of ice cream for the following week."

"I can think of a good way to work off the calories and keep you distracted," Tim said.

"I am not doing any extra workouts," she snapped.

"Let me amend my statement, counselor." Tim unbuttoned her blouse. "I can think of a much better way to work off the calories and keep you distracted."

And he did until the intercom by the front door of the loft buzzed.

Harri gently pressed her hands against his chest. "Wait. That may be important."

"Steve was going to a law school party tonight," Tim murmured. "He's probably drunk and hit the wrong button."

She frowned. "While I'm glad you're taking your superhero retirement seriously, I did go to law school, and it's way too early for him to be home." The obnoxious buzz filled their loft again. "We'd better check."

Her phone started warbling the Dolly Parton tune, "Nine to Five".

"That's not a drunk Steve." She yanked the phone out of her jacket pocket and tapped the answer icon. "What's wrong, Patty?"

Patty Ames, their legal assistant and all-around Girl Friday, sounded terribly worried. "Turn on Channel 12. There's a special report. One of our twins got busted for flying in his civvies at Canyon Pointe University."

Harri's fingers tightened around her phone as she launched herself from the bed and charged into the living room. It was a good thing she hadn't turned off the lamp on the end table then she came home tonight. She grabbed the remote and turned on the TV. Tim had programmed the channel into the quick buttons after Aisha became the station's on-air legal commentator during the summer.

Shaky video appeared to show a Christmas party at the Madison Hotel's rooftop restaurant, but it was the action in the background that worried Harri. A person in a hoodie and jeans stood on the exterior ledge of the roof for the Hardwick Building which housed the Canyon Pointe University Law School. Harri's heart lodged in her throat.

A jumper.

Someone with dark hair leaned on the retaining wall near the jumper. The attention of the partiers at the hotel were drawn to the drama by someone pointing it out. The figure in the hoodie started to turn toward the person with them.

The jumper jerked as if startled, then they were falling. And the second person literally dived over the roof. The folks at the hotel party screamed. A fraction of a second later, both people from the law school reappeared in the video. The dark-haired person obviously flew as he carried the jumper back to the roof.

Harri looked up at Tim who had followed her into the living room. "I told you Steve wasn't home this early."

CHAPTER 3

◆━━━◆◆◆━━━◆

Aisha Franklin's phone vibrated on the side table. She sighed and hit the pause button on the remote. Dang it. Her son went down without a fuss, and she and Rey were cuddled on the couch, watching a sci-fi movie, after a horrible interview with a potential associate.

"It's late. You could let it go to voicemail," her husband said.

She picked up the phone and checked the caller ID. "It's Harri, and she's not pounding on the door and waking Mitch. So I will be civil and answer her." She flicked the appropriate icon on her smart phone. "What's wrong, girl? You still pissed about the interview."

"This isn't about the jackass. Turn on the Action 12! News twenty-four-hour channel." Harri sighed. "Your brother-in-law is on camera doing something he shouldn't be doing in public."

"Please be drunk, Steve," Aisha whispered as she switched from the movie streaming service to the news channel. "Please be drunk."

Sure enough, Ted Meadowfield's voice spoke over the amateur video onscreen. ". . . unknown super rescued a jumper. We haven't been able to reach anyone at Canyon Pointe University for comment, but according to the law school's website, the student council scheduled a post-finals party tonight at the Margaret Jackson Patio on the roof of the Hardwick Building which houses the law school. Ted Meadowfield. Action 12! News."

The camera switched back to Brian Mason, the backup evening anchor, at the studio. "Thank you, Ted. We'll be updating this story throughout the night as more information comes in. We'll be back with this week's weather report after these short messages from our sponsors."

Rey mumbled a few choice obscenities as he scowled at the screen.

"Have you spoken with Steve yet?" Aisha asked her law partner.

"No," Harri answered. "What do I tell him? Especially after Rey saved my ass in the same manner before he registered? That Steve should have let the kid splatter on the concrete?"

"Put it on speaker." Rey gestured at Aisha's phone. She tapped the necessary icon. "Harri, do you want me to head down to the school and pick up Steve?"

"We do not need Black Falcon pulled into this mess," Harri snapped.

"I was going to take the minivan," Rey said dryly. "We registered it in Aisha's name only for a reason. It's not going to raise as many questions if an attorney picks up a client who accidentally outed himself."

"If we're going that route, I should be the one who goes to retrieve him," Aisha murmured.

"What about Steve's truck?" Tim's voice crackled through the speaker.

Aisha exchanged a look with her husband. When Miguel Esperanza, their building manager replaced his work truck, Steve had bought the ancient red pickup because he didn't want to stand out among the students at the law school. She knew exactly how the other students regarded the trust-fund babies, even though Steve's adoptive parents were new money, not old like Harri and Tim's families.

"I'll grab Emilio," Rey said. "I've got Steve's spare keys."

"Then go," Harri said. "Aisha and I will brainstorm some damage control."

"Can you please come over here?" Aisha asked.

"I wasn't going to make you wake Mitch and bring him across the hall," Harri grumbled. "Come over to our loft and bring the baby monitor with you so I don't wake him."

Aisha chuckled. "You plan on getting loud?"

"Not on purpose."

"I'll be over in a minute." Aisha tapped the icon to end the call.

Rey kissed her before he rose from the couch. "I'll go get my shoes and keys. We'll finish our movie tomorrow night."

But something deep inside said Aisha would never see the end of the movie until she and Rey returned from Paris next December.

CHAPTER 4

⬥ ● ⬥

Steve's gut twisted as he touched down on the law school's roof patio with Mariah in his arms. All the other students stared at him. A few even had out their phones, no doubt taking both still pictures as well as video.

At the forefront of the crowd stood his friends. Bethany and Nick stared at him with open mouths. Carter, however, scowled at him.

"Mariah," Steve whispered. "We're back on the roof. Do you think you can stand?"

Her eyes were still squeezed tight, and she shook her head vigorously against his chest.

Carter charged toward him. "What the fuck, man? All the crap you give me about being rich, and you're a super?"

"I do not give you crap," Steve growled through clenched teeth. "And now is definitely not the time for this discussion."

"Get me out of here." Mariah's words were followed by a sob.

Dammit, he couldn't leave her alone. And he couldn't do a thing about all the witnesses either. So, he did what he usually did when faced with a major problem. He plowed forward.

The other students parted to let Mariah and him pass.

"Steve, wait." Bethany caught up with them. "You're going to need some help tonight." He hated to admitted, she was right. Mariah need more help than he knew how to give, and Aisha would be chewing him a new one for displaying his powers in public the minute she found out. He just hoped he'd be the one to tell her.

He gave Bethany a curt nod. "Come on."

She rushed ahead of him and Mariah and opened the stairwell door. Pounding footsteps and gasping breath announced Nick's presence.

"I'm coming with you guys," he said.

"Is that okay, Mariah?" Steve murmured.

She clutched his shirt and whimpered, "Just don't let me go."

Steve glanced over his shoulder. The other students continued to stare at him, and no one spoke a word, even among themselves. That settled any indecision he had. He headed down the stairs.

"I'll drive your truck," Nick said as he and Bethany jogged after Steve. "You need to focus on her."

"Are you saying girls can't drive trucks?" Bethany bit out.

"I know damn well you can't drive a manual transmission," Nick shot back. "I can. You take my car and follow us."

Once they were out of the building and in the parking lot, Bethany dug into Steve's pocket for his keys and traded them for Nick's set. Bethany whirled and raced for Nick's car two rows over from the truck. Nick made sure Steve and Mariah were settled in the passenger seat of the pickup before he carefully shut the door, ran around to the driver side and slid into the seat.

"Wait," Steve said right before Nick turned the ignition. "How much have you had to drink? Last thing either of us need is to get picked up for DUI."

"Only a couple of swallows from my cup before you arrived." Nick started the truck and shot Steve a look. "I am not Carter."

"Never said you were." Steve reached behind the seat and grabbed the emergency blanket. Mariah shivered so hard her teeth chattered. However, the city retained so much of the day's heat, the temperatures were still in the high seventies. Which meant she was going into shock.

Steve wrapped Mariah in the blanket and held her tight in his right arm while he tugged his phone out of his pocket with his left hand. He scrolled through his contacts and tapped Serena's number.

The line rang three times before Serena mumbled, "This better be good, Connors."

He quickly explained the situation with Mariah's threat to jump and how he talked her off the ledge.

"*Ese*, you need to take her to the ER," she said. "I don't do mental health issues."

Crap. He wanted to avoid the rest of the truth, but Serena wouldn't be as ticked off as Aisha.

"I can't," he said through gritted teeth. "She started to climb back onto the roof and slipped. I had to use my powers to save her, and she's so freaked by the partial fall I think she's going into shock, which is a physical issue."

"Oh, my god," Serena whispered. "Did anyone see you?"

"Yes," he bit out. "Make a left on MLK," he said to Nick. Thankfully, his fellow student focused on the streets and traffic, and he didn't ask questions.

Yet, anyway. Steve knew Nick and Bethany would demand answers later.

"Who's with you?" Serena demanded.

"A friend I trust to keep his mouth shut," Steve barked. "Can you help this girl or not?"

"I'll meet you at Lechuza," Serena snapped back. The line went dead.

"She's intense," Nick commented.

"Not as intense as my girlfriend." Despite the quip, Steve could visualize Qiang's reaction. She was a fiercely private person. When the story got out about his rescue of Mariah, she wouldn't just chew him out like Aisha would.

No, Qiang would electrocute him.

CHAPTER 5

Harri stepped out of the elevator, Rey and Emilio Esperanza, the son of their building manager, on her heels. She claimed she came down to reset the security alarm after the guys left, but she really wanted to check the street for paparazzi. Despite all their precautions, Meadowfield would discover Steve's local address.

Some way, some how.

However, she jerked to a stop when she spotted Serena Alvarez staring at them through the bullet-proof glass of the side door to the garage. The student physician's assistant held up her hand as if she was about to hit the building's intercom. Rey punched in the code to deactivate the Lechuza Building's security system and pushed open the door.

Serena strode inside, her backpack slung over her shoulder. "Did I beat Steve here?"

"You've talked to him?" Harri asked.

"Yeah, he called me." Serena's white eyebrows formed a deep V in her dark skin. "He said he had a classmate he talked down from committing suicide by concrete. She slipped anyway and he saved her from the plummet, but now she's going into shock."

"That would explain why he hasn't answered our calls," Rey said dryly.

"Whether he's driving or flying back here, I'd prefer he pays attention to what he's doing," Harri commented.

"He's in a vehicle with another friend driving him." Serena shook her head. "I tried to talk him into taking her to the hospital, but he said he couldn't. There were extenuating circumstances. He asked me to meet him here."

"That may be the first smart thing he's done tonight," Harri growled.

"Does this mean I can go back to bed?" Emilio asked.

"Yeah, man." Rey clapped him on the shoulder. "Sorry, I got you up for nothing."

"De nada." A wry smile crossed Emilio's face. ""For once, it didn't involve supervillains or heroes gone bad. See you at work tomorrow." He took a step toward the elevator and looked back at the three standing by the door. "I hope the girl's okay."

"So do we," Harri said.

The distinctive sounds of the gates opening and closing wafted past the grand staircase to the second and third floors. No one standing by the side door spoke until their antique elevator ground to a halt on the fourth floor.

Harri looked up at Rey. "You going to give him shit?"

He folded his arms across his chest. "No. Steve's probably kicking himself enough right now." He exhaled wearily. "He just wanted a normal life." A wry smile crossed his face. "It's the one thing I understood about him."

Harri didn't know what to say. For the last year and a half, Rey carried a lot of resentment when it came to his twin brother. The odd part? That resentment wasn't focused on Steve's well-to-do adoptive parents. It was the fact that Steve had a family, instead of growing up on the streets and being chased by monsters and the defunct black-ops group Corvus like Rey had been his entire life.

"That's all anyone wants," Harri murmured.

"And yet, everyone else would kill for our lives." Serena laughed bitterly.

"If they could experience both sides, I think you'd be surprised how many would choose the non-powered life," Rey said.

"Like who?" Serena muttered.

"Aisha," he said.

Harri leaned against the door frame. "That depends on whether she can keep you and Mitch because she wouldn't trade you two for anything."

Dark rose flushed Rey's face. "Honestly, if I had to choose between my powers and my family, I'd definitely chose my family."

Serena chuckled. "You both sound like my mama."

"Family's the most important thing." Harri smiled before she glanced at Rey. "Sometimes, it's blood. Sometimes, it's found family. Either way, it's damn important."

Tires screeched outside. Harri pushed away from the door jamb and turned in time to see Steve's red truck whiz by the side entrance. A blue compact sedan followed.

"Where are they going?" Harri muttered.

"The last row in the garage behind the pillars." Rey scowled. "It's bad if Steve's that worried about someone spotting his truck from the street."

Speak of the devil. Steve raced toward the door, carrying someone wrapped in a thermal emergency blanket. Two other twenty-somethings ran after him.

Harri shoved the door open, but once Steve entered, she stepped in front of the male and female following. "Who are you two?"

"We're with Steve and Mariah," the girl blurted.

"Harri, that's Nick Lyons and Bethany Spears," Steve said. "They're part of my study group. They know about me, and they know what happened to Mariah."

"I hate to tell you this, bro," Rey said. "Nearly everyone in Canyon Pointe knows about you now."

Steve grimaced. "That's just peachy. Mariah needs Serena to check her out. We'll deal with the rest after that."

Harri eyed the two law students. "If you two step out of line while you're in my building, I won't need a super. I'll dispose of you myself. *Capisce?*"

"Y-you're Harri Winters!" the kid Steve called Nick said.

"Let's get my patient upstairs, then you can threaten the law students, Harri." Serena smirked.

"Take her up to my place," Harri ordered. She snapped her fingers and pointed at the retreating backs of the twins. "You two, get in here. And don't you dare repeat anything you hear or see."

"Yes, ma'am," both kids muttered. They trotted after Rey, Steve, and the suicidal Mariah.

"I don't know if this is a good idea," Serena muttered. "I've spent my life trying to stay off everyone's radar."

"Then let's hope the partners here have enough clout to keep these two quiet about all of us," Harri growled.

However, Rey was right. Action 12! News had already shown one amateur video of the incident. How many more would pour in from Steve's classmates before tomorrow morning?

CHAPTER 6

"What the hell were you thinking?" Aisha shouted. She glanced at the baby monitor sitting on Harri's kitchen island. Not a peep from Mitch. Normally, she wouldn't yell at someone in front of witnesses, but she couldn't yell at her brother-in-law in her own place without waking the baby.

Steve stared back at her. "What did you want me to do? Let Mariah splatter all over the pavement?"

Harri laughed, and Tim snickered.

Aisha whirled to face them. "This isn't funny! We have a serious problem here!"

"Don't forget dragging his friends into this mess," Rey said.

"You are not helping," Steve growled.

Aisha glared at the two law students quivering on Harri's turquoise couch. "Give Tim your phones."

The girl held up her hands. "We didn't film Steve. I swear!"

"Then you don't have any reason not to give our head of security your phones to double-check." Aisha smiled sweetly at the pair.

"Don't argue with her." Steve sighed. "When she gets nice, it means she's about to make you do what she wants."

"But you have super powers," the boy murmured, his attention flicking from person to person.

"I'm going to double-check you two don't have any evidence regarding Steve's abilities on your phones." Tim strode over to the pair and held out his hands. "I'm also going to check to make sure you aren't carrying any spyware on your phones. I'll also install some protective software. If you're friends with Steve, you could be targeted by some not-so-friendly people."

"I knew it," Nick blurted. "You secretly wear your underwear in public."

"No," Aisha snapped. "He's a member of our firm's staff. Not every super runs around in their underwear!"

"You need to chill, girl," Harri said softly.

"Why aren't you taking this seriously—"

Harri seemed a little shorter than normal.

Aisha flexed her feet. Nothing met her bare toes but air. Great. Just great. She closed her eyes, swallowed hard, and concentrated. Her soles met Harri's hardwood floor again.

"Why don't you check on the baby?" Rey said softly. "You can beat Steve over the head with a tree tomorrow."

Aisha folded her arms over her chest. "That's not funny either."

But her husband was right. She was not handling this situation well. Especially when this was the second time in the last four months, she'd accidentally revealed her own powers.

There was a knock on Harri's door before it rolled back. Susan Kennedy, their third partner, entered the loft, dressed in her jammies which featured a certain Japanese feline in bright pink.

"I'm assuming you've seen the news," she said.

"Yeah, but we've got to assume the blurry video isn't the only one," Aisha said.

"Crap." Susan ran her fingers through her red locks. "You haven't seen the latest, have you?"

"The latest?" Aisha's heart sank.

"A bunch of students at the law school named Steve as the super and provided their own videos," Susan said. "Ted's practically dancing in glee on the twenty-four-seven news channel."

"Shit!" Harri started pacing. "It's a matter of time before they show up on our front door. Why didn't Nella give us a heads-up?"

"Because she was probably at home, and Delacorte made the call," Aisha muttered. The assistant news producer wasn't deliberately malicious, but he would have caved to Ted's demands to air the footage.

"It won't just be our front door." Steve threw his hands in the air. "What about my parents? Oh, my god, why did I ever join the Peace Corps? If I hadn't gone to Honduras—"

"Stop it!" Aisha marched over to him. "Stop second-guessing yourself. It happened. We'll deal. Like you said, you couldn't let Mariah die."

She turned to Nick and Bethany. "You two. Give Tim your phones now."

They obeyed without question. Tim strode past Susan and out the loft door.

"Not that I'm trying to get out of damage control," Susan said. "But I do have a trial first thing in the morning."

"Go. Take care of Amperage." Harri waved her hand in a shooing motion. "We've got this."

Once Susan left, Aisha eyed Harri. "Are you sure we have this?"

"We'd better," Harri growled.

Aisha bit her tongue to keep from spilling her own fears. With Steve outed, it was only a matter of time before her carefully constructed new superhero identity for her husband would fall apart under the searing glare of the press.

And that would give the U.S. government their excuse for taking Mitch away from her and Rey.

CHAPTER 7

Air froze in Steve's lungs when Serena entered Harri's living room with an awful expression. "How's Mariah?"

"She's asleep." The healer pursed her lips. "There's a reason for her depression."

"Yeah, her parents are putting a ton of pressure on her—"

"It's more than that." Serena exhaled. "She's got a brain tumor."

"What?" Bethany sprang up from her place on the couch. "What are you talking about?"

"Can you help her?" Steve asked.

"That's not how my abilities work." A tear trickled down Serena's cheek, and she swiped it away. "It's cancer. Her own cells. My power accelerates the healing of an injury or an illness. If I even tried to help her, I'd kill her."

"Did you tell her?" Harri asked.

Serena nodded. "And I already called Doctor O'Brien. She will get Mariah consultations with a neurologist and an oncologist in the morning, but . . ." She hugged herself and shook her head.

Aisha walked over and wrapped an arm around her. "It's not your fault, girl. Don't beat yourself up over this."

"Thank you for coming, Serena," Steve said. "If you hadn't looked at her tonight, she might not have found out about the tumor until it was too late."

Serena nodded, but the morose air continued to surround her.

"Do you need a ride home?" Rey asked.

That shook the healer out of her own depressed state. "I live four doors down from you guys."

Nick rose from Harri's couch. "I'll walk you down to your place."

"Thanks, but I'll do it," Rey said.

"I can handle myself," Nick argued.

Steve stepped between his friend and his brother. "I know you can, but the folks on this street are pretty tight. They see a stranger, they have a tendency to jump to conclusions."

"And you get a pass because he's your brother?" Bethany inclined her head toward Rey.

Steve glanced at Rey behind him before he turned back to his study partners. "Actually, yes."

"Let's get you home." Rey beckoned Serena.

Once they left, Aisha stepped closer to Steve. "I'm sorry for yelling at you like I did."

"You didn't know," he replied softly. "And you're right. I outed myself. I need to call Mom and Dad and warn them." The real reason his sister-in-law was upset struck home. "I would never deliberately put Rey and Mitch at risk, Aisha. You've got to know that."

"I know you wouldn't do something intentionally," she said. "But, we've got a hell of a mess to deal with tomorrow. All of us need to get some sleep."

She turned to Bethany and Nick. "It might be best if you two spent the night here. If you've been seen with Steve publicly, you're going to be harassed by the press for the next few days until some other story hits."

"Nick can stay in my spare bedroom if it's all right Bethany stays in yours," Steve said.

"I was going to suggest the same thing." Aisha smiled at Bethany. "As long as you can deal with a baby who I can guarantee will be up by six a.m."

Bethany held up her hands with her fingers spread. "As long as I don't have to change diapers, we're good."

"Then all of you, out," Harri ordered. "I need some sleep myself in order to deal with this mess in the morning."

In his apartment on the third floor, Steve showed the extra bedroom and the separate bath to Nick. "Towels are in the cupboard. Extra toothbrushes and toothpaste are in the top drawer of the vanity. If you need anything else—"

"We need to have a serious talk, man," Nick said. "You said you were living with your brother and sister-in-law and interning for her in return for room and board. You left a hell of a lot out of your story."

The muscles in Steve's neck and back tensed. "I didn't lie to you."

"No, you just didn't tell us everything. Like your sister-in-law is Aisha Franklin." Nick shook his head. "Was it because of Carter? I know he can lord his family's money and so-called prestige over everyone."

"What? No!" Steve protested. In fact, Carter's behavior made him take a good hard look at his own. He hadn't been that much different from Carter before Professor Paranoia kidnapped him and screwed with his mind.

"Got anything to drink?" Nick asked.

"Just soda, tea, and juice." Steve cocked his head.

"Some ice tea sounds good right now." Nick eyed him. "And you're going to tell me the rest of the story."

Steve blew out a deep breath and rubbed the back of his neck. "I'll tell you what I can, but a lot of it is governed under attorney-client privilege."

"You're not a lawyer yet." Nick smirked.

"But Aisha is, she's also my boss, and she'd kick my ass." Steve turned and headed for the kitchen.

"Let me guess," Nick said from behind him. "She developed HRSP while she was pregnant, and it didn't go away."

"That's not my story to tell," Steve retorted.

"Dude, she was levitating in the middle of Ms. Winters' living room." Nick chuckled.

"All right." Steve flung his arms in the air as they entered the kitchen. "It was HRSP."

"Thank you," Nick said. "Now, do you got any snacks, too?"

"How heavy do you want?" Steve asked. "I've got anything from a lasagna in the freezer to potato chips and dip."

"Let's stick with the chips and dip." Nick laughed. "Though if I have to hide here through the holiday break, I'll take you up on the lasagna."

Steve winced. While he was glad Nick and Bethany were taking this mess in stride, how would they feel if they couldn't spend the holidays with their families? They might not be so happy about things.

"Did you have any big plans for the break?" Steve asked while he retrieved glasses from the cupboard.

"Christmas dinner at Grandma's." Nick perched on one of the bar stools. "You?"

"I was supposed to fly up to Mom and Dad's—shit!" Steve pulled his phone from his pocket. "Let me call my parents." He pointed at the pantry. "Potato chips are in there. Top shelf."

Nick slid off the stool and retrieved the unopened bag while Steve tapped the speed dial for Mom's cell phone number. Thank goodness, Seattle was an hour behind Canyon Pointe. Mom and Dad should still be awake.

"Hey, sweetie!" Mom chirped. "I didn't expect to hear from you tonight."

"I know, but something's happened." Steve sucked in a deep breath.

Mom must have put her phone on speaker because Dad's deep voice said, "What happened, Steve? Are you okay?"

"I'm fine." He licked his lips and spilled the story of the end-of-finals party and Mariah's fall. "The end result is not only were there witnesses, but I was caught on camera flying, and I've already been identified to the press by some of my classmates."

"But your friend is all right, isn't she?" Mom asked.

"As well as can be expected," he said. "One of our neighbors who's a physician's assistant checked Mariah over. Harri and Tim are watching her tonight. Then Doctor O'Brien is getting referrals for her so she can get the right kind of help."

"What did Aisha say about all this?" Dad asked.

Steve chuckled. "After she chewed me a new asshole, she said to get some sleep, and we'd deal with it in the morning."

"Don't take her anger personally, sweetie," Mom said. "She's worried about that precious little baby of hers."

"Believe me, I know." He'd been researching cases for Harri where the government took super children from their parents and their various justifications for doing so. The history made him realize he was damn lucky the Feds hadn't come for him.

And how easy it would be for Rey and Aisha to lose Mitch.

Steve scratched his forehead. "Look, I just wanted to warn you that news people may be on your front lawn tonight."

"We can deal with them," Dad said. "Be careful, and listen to Aisha and Harri for Mitch's sake if not for yours."

"I will," he promised. "I love you both."

"We love you, too," his parents chorused.

Steve ended the call and looked at Nick. "No snarky comments?"

"Dude, tonight, Mariah's parents almost ended up having to give their daughter a closed casket funeral," Nick said. "I'm not about to give you shit for telling your mom and dad you love them."

Steve opened the freezer compartment and scooped ice into the two glasses. He retrieved the pitcher of tea he'd made earlier this afternoon. After pouring some into each of the two glasses, he handed one glass to Nick and set his glass and the pitcher on the island. He had a feeling they'd empty it tonight.

No sooner had he grabbed the container of French onion dip and claimed a stool on the opposite side of the island from Nick, there was a soft knock on his apartment door.

"Come in."

Rey entered. "Thought I'd better warn you. There's already TV trucks in front of the building."

"Crap," Steve muttered. "Did they give you shit?"

"Nah, I came in through Celia's." Which meant he'd cut through the old, unused subway tunnel beneath this block and entered through the Lechuza Building's basement. It also meant the reporters and their crew never saw him.

Rey closed the apartment door. "Mind if I join you for a bit?"

"Avoiding the missus?" Nick asked.

"Actually, checking on my brother." Rey approached the island. "Can I have some of that ice tea?"

For some reason, the request pleased Steve. He'd always wanted a sibling, but Mom and Dad's efforts to adopt another child fell through for one reason or another. Professor Paranoia and Corvus's actions had ensured Rey's resentment of him. And really, he couldn't blame his twin for that resentment. He'd ruined the reputation of Rey's first superhero persona Captain Justice and nearly killed Tim who was Rey's mentor.

Steve grinned. "Sure you don't want a Mexican orange soda?"

"That's even better." Rey claimed the stool next to Nick. "I'm sorry Aisha gave you a rough time tonight, but you did the right thing by saving Mariah."

Steve retrieved the bottle of soda from his refrigerator, removed the cap, and handed it to his brother. "She has every right to be angry with me. My fuck-up put you and Mitch in danger of discovery."

"We're heading to Europe in a few weeks. In a year, this will blow over." Rey shrugged and took a swig of his soda.

Steve snorted. "What are you suggesting? I take a year off from law school?"

"Dude, are you really telling him to run away from his problems?" Nick shook his head. "Is that what Black Falcon would tell any of his fans?"

Steve froze. Of course, Nick figured out the truth. So would Bethany. Neither of them were stupid.

However, Rey tried to play off Nick's question. "Black Falcon? You couldn't come up with a better superhero example?"

"There are only two superheroes in Canyon Pointe with Steve's skill set of strength, speed, and flight." Nick grabbed a potato chip from the bag. "And that's Black Falcon and Captain Mojave." He pointed to Steve and Rey in turn with the chip. "And you're both too young to be Captain Mojave. Now, if you were the Ghost Owl, then Steve would have been able to turn invisible, too, and none of Mariah's rescue would have been a problem."

Nick plunged his chip in the French onion dip and shoved it into his mouth. His expression dared Steve and Rey to argue with him.

"All right," Rey said. "What do you want to keep your mouth shut?"

"I don't want anything from either of you." Nick grabbed another chip. "Though it would totally suck if Steve has to leave Canyon Pointe University after this." He dragged the chip through the dip. "But I admit I'm being partly selfish. He's the reason I made it through this semester."

Steve's phone jittered across the granite top of the island. He looked at the caller ID. "It's Carter."

"Who?" Rey asked.

"Carter Swift," Steve said. "He's the only member of our study group not here tonight."

"You want me to handle it?" Nick asked.

"No, thanks." Steve breathed a little sigh of relief Rey hadn't jumped in with an opinion. Or a demand to solve the problem. He thumbed the answer icon. "Hey, Carter."

"You bastard," Carter hissed. "I'm reporting you for cheating."

"Cheating?" Steve glanced at Rey who motioned for him to record the call. With a tap, the red light in the corner of the phone's screen glowed. "Can you say that again Carter? You broke up. It sounded like you were accusing me of cheating."

"You used your superpowers to cheat," Carter yelled.

"How are you coming to that conclusion?" Steve eyed Rey who was texting something on his own phone.

"I don't care how you did it, but I know you did," Carter spat. "I'm not the only one who thinks so, and we've already left messages with the dean. You are going down, Connors!" The line went dead.

CHAPTER 8

After a godawful interview and then Steve accidentally outing himself as a super, Harri decided to take a hot bath with lavender essential oil before bed. She didn't realize how relaxed she was in the tub until someone knocked on the bathroom door. She jerked, and water sloshed over the edges of the antique claw-foot tub. Thank goodness, Miguel insisted on ceramic tiles in the bathrooms when he was rehabbing the building.

Tim peered around the edge of the partly open door. "Didn't mean to startle you."

"You wouldn't have interrupted if it wasn't important." She waved for him to come in. "Is Mariah okay?"

"She's still asleep." Tim perched on Harri's vanity stool. "Rey's back. He said there's already a couple of news vans parked at our front door."

"That's to be expected." Harri grimaced. "Someone at the school probably accessed Steve's current address." She leaned her head back against the rim of the tub. "I was hoping we'd have a little more time before they started hounding us here."

"Steve also got a threatening call from one of his study group," Tim added.

Harri frowned. "I thought they were all here because of Mariah."

"Apparently, Mariah was not part of his study group." Tim leaned his elbows on his knees. "There's another student named Carter Swift. Apparently, he's a trust fund baby."

"Great," Harri muttered. "So he's one of 'our' people."

"Steve's done a great job of trying to fit in with the middle class majority at the law school." Tim grinned. "Probably too good."

"Wait a minute." Harri sat upright, sloshing more water over the tub edges. "Is he any relation to Mojave Supreme Court Justice Channing Swift?"

"Let's find out." Tim pulled his phone from his pocket. Harri's bath water noticeably cooled while she waited for an answer.

"Justice Swift does have a twenty-three-year-old grandson named Carter." Tim looked up at her. "Think it's the same kid?"

Harri snorted as she climbed to her feet and stepped over the edge of the tub. "I think young Mr. Swift should reconsider threatening people." She reached for her towel. "It would be better if we had more than Steve's say-so about Carter's threat."

Tim grinned in a way that had nothing to do with her current state on undress.

"He recorded the call?" Harri's eyebrows climbed her forehead.

"According to Rey, he did." Tim slipped his phone in his pocket before he stood and took the towel from her.

"Well, hot damn. The kids actually listened to me." She relaxed a bit, more from Tim gently drying her skin than from Steve following her advice.

"We need to have a staff meeting first thing in the morning," Tim murmured.

She groaned. "You're about to add new security measures and restrictions for the staff."

"If it were just the press we needed to worry about, I wouldn't." Tim tossed aside the towel and pulled her back against his chest. "But this Carter thing could escalate, and there's Mariah to be concerned about. She doesn't need the pressure of public scrutiny while she deals with her health issues."

"Tonight's crap is going to put a crimp in finding another associate before New Year's," she said.

"That's three weeks away, Harri." Tim chuckled softly in her ear. "You were never going to hire anyone before the beginning of the year."

"I wanted to. I tried to," she whined. Crap, she hated when she did that, but with Tim, she finally felt she could let her guard down, and he wouldn't use her weakness against her. "I thought if I did, we could go to Vegas and get married on January First."

"That's really what you want to do?" he asked.

She turned around to face him. "I want our wedding to be fun. Not utilitarian. Not some big formal event. Aisha and Rey's ceremony was the best time I ever had at a penguin party. And this way, we could do it before the Franklin-Garcias head to Europe."

"There's no reason we can't still do that." Tim grinned.

Harri shook her head. "If we don't figure out how to fix Steve's problem first, the press will eat him alive before we can get him on a plane to Sin City."

CHAPTER 9

The next morning, Aisha volunteered Rey to watch both Mitch and Grace down at Patty and Arthur's apartment in order for Bethany to get some extra sleep. She remembered all too well staying in bed for twenty-four hours straight after finals each semester of law school.

Rather than possibly wake the sleepers up by taking the elevator, she took the stairs. When she reached the third floor landing and opened the door, only the deep breathing sounds of two people sleeping filtered down the hallway. The extra sleep would do Steve and Nick some good, too. She gently closed the stairwell door and continued down to the first floor.

The glass on the side door was nearly black with the privacy film Arthur had created. A nine-volt battery's charge made the normally transparent plastic better than the best light blocking shades or curtains. Good for protecting the occupants of the building from mobs and snipers.

Not so good for her. She needed natural light to wake up in the morning. She'd been that way long before she met Rey and got her powers.

Harri came out of the breakroom with her cinnamon-laced coffee as Aisha entered the reception area. "Staff meeting at nine, and no one is to leave the building. We've already got every news van in the Canyon Pointe metro area sitting on our doorstep. So far, they are behaving themselves."

Well, that explained why the privacy film had been activated.

"Rey told me we had some campers last night." Aisha glanced at the main doors. They were dark, too. "I hate having to leave my blinds closed." She turned back to Harri. "How's Susan going to get to court?"

"Already called the CPPD about the traffic issues, and Cobblestone is on his way over to keep the garage entrance clear." Harri slurped her coffee.

"Have you called Travis?"

Harri nodded. "I told him to work from home for today. He relishes media attention about as much as I do. Have you talked to Dejon?"

"I told him I was giving him a paid day off considering the circumstances," Aisha said. "Molly said she'd come in to watch the kids this afternoon. Emilio and Rey plan to use the tunnels to get to work, but how are we going to get Mariah to any medical appointments?"

Harri sipped her coffee before she said, "You or Rey are going to have to take her through the tunnels as well. Unless the Ghost Owl or Black Falcon plans on flying out one of the windows with cameras trained on every exposed inch of the building."

"That's not funny," Aisha snapped.

Harri shrugged. "The alternative is taking her in somebody's minivan, and we keep her face covered. This kind of crap is why I'm not a fan of the Fourth Estate."

"They have their uses . . ." Aisha cocked her head. Something was off in the reception area. She looked around her. No one else was down here yet, but it was only seven-thirty. The real reason for the extra quiet finally hit her.

"Why aren't the firm lines ringing?" she asked.

"I left them on voice-mail." Harri shook her head. "It is too damn early to deal with reporters, and I hadn't had my coffee yet."

Almost as if to make them both liars, Aisha's cell phone warbled. She pulled it from her jacket pocket. "Crap, it's Nella."

"You can't avoid your boss forever." Harri smirked.

"Just because I'm Action 12!'s legal commentator—" The phone stopped ringing for a second, then started again. This was one of the few times she wished she hadn't taken the job at the TV station.

Aisha sucked in a deep breath and tapped the answer icon. "Couldn't you let me get my coffee first?"

"Well, yippie-ki-ay to you, too, Aisha," Action 12!'s news producer snapped.

"I'm sorry," Aisha said. "I'm trying to get my ducks lined up before we leave next month, but I swear the universe is throwing stuff at me faster than I clear it off my desk. What do you need?"

"I actually called to warn you. Ted's on the rampage."

Aisha chuckled. "What else is new?"

"He bullied Reed Delacorte and bypassed both me and Mark." Nella audibly gulped. "He went straight to Mr. Riggs and pitched the story that Captain Justice was still alive."

Being the son-in-law of the station's owner was the only reason Ted hadn't been fired for any of his dumbass moves. Breaking a story of this magnitude would redeem Ted in Mr. Riggs's eyes.

However, Aisha couldn't catch her breath. Maybe it was a good thing she hadn't had coffee yet after all. She would have vomited all over the floor at Nella's news. Her nightmares were coming true.

"That's-that's totally ridiculous," she forced past the acid in her throat.

"That's what I told Mr. Riggs." Nella sighed. "He said either the story will get Ted a spot at a major network or the law student's own attorney will force the station to fire Ted."

"He's setting up his own son-in-law?" Aisha asked incredulously.

Nella snorted. "You know Holland will beg her daddy to change his mind, and Mr. Riggs will give in. I suggest using your contract to protect this Steve kid. And I wouldn't blame you for quitting over this. I'm really sorry."

"What all does Ted know so far?"

Nella rattled off all of Steve's pertinent facts: age, education, his kidnapping in Honduras, his adoptive parents' names and address. She finished with his current address.

Which of course was the Lechuza Building.

"Does this kid even want to be a super?" Nella asked.

"No, he really doesn't," Aisha said. "That's why he's in law school."

"Tell him I'm sorry, and I'll let you know if Ted gets any closer to doing something stupid." Nella paused for a second before she added, "I'm serious. Use your contract to shut this down before Ted ruins this kid's life."

Aisha ended the call and slipped her phone back in her jacket pocket.

"How bad?" Harri asked.

"Ted thinks Steve is Captain Justice, and he faked his death."

"But he hasn't connected him to Rey yet, has he?"

Aisha shook her head. "Nella suggested I go after Ted and the station for harassing our intern."

A malicious grin spread across Harri's face. "I need to send Nella a very nice present for the holidays this year. Do you mind if I take the lead on this?"

"Knock yourself out." Aisha smirked. For once, she was ecstatic over her law partner's vindictive streak. "Merry Christmas."

CHAPTER 10

Steve sat on his couch and stared at the Action 12! News on the TV as he nibbled on one of the omelets Rey had left for him and Nick in the refrigerator. After all the resentment his brother had cast in his direction once they found out about each, it was a little weird with Rey being so frickin' polite and doing shit for him. But damn, his twin could cook.

Of course, the accusations Ted Meadowfield was throwing probably had more to do with Rey's behavior. The idiot reporter seemed absolutely sure Steve was Captain Justice, and he had faked his death to avoid prosecution for the murder of the original Ghost Owl.

From what Harri had told Steve, the Channel 12 anchor had it in for Rey before he even donned the Captain Justice moniker. Something about Rey putting Ted's beloved Corvette in a place where he had to shell out some serious bucks to get it down without severely damaging it. Her story proved Rey had a sense of humor at one point.

Nick shuffled into the living room, wearing some extra sweats and a t-shirt Steve had loaned him. He looked at the big screen, then at Steve. "Turn it off, man. Meadowfield's an idiot, and his BS is only going to drive you crazy."

His friend was right. Steve thumbed the remote, the screen winked off, and he immediately felt a little better without Meadowfield's grating voice.

"There's a bacon, spinach, and Swiss omelet in the fridge for you," Steve said. "Bread, English muffins, and bagels are in the cupboard above the toaster."

"You trying to prove something here?" Nick's right eyebrow rose.

"Like what?"

"Not only are you top of the class, you're cooking for me?"

Steve shook his head. "Nope. That's my brother. The short order cook who wants to become a gourmet chef."

Nick chuckled as he retrieved his breakfast from the refrigerator. "I don't think I've personally known any supers until I met you. You and your family are not what I expected."

"What did you expect?" Steve asked.

"Secret lairs. Supervillain smackdowns." Nick popped the plate into the microwave and set the timer before he turned to Steve and grinned. "Orgies with super chicks in piles of the licensing money you bring in."

"I don't bring in any licensing money," Steve insisted.

"But you could make a ton more money as a bona fide superhero than you could as an attorney." Nick pulled out the bagels before he turned back to Steve with a stunned expression. "Oh, my god! You're dating a superhero, aren't you? That's the real reason you won't introduce us to her."

"Actually, the issue is she's older than me." Steve shrugged. "The age difference makes her uncomfortable."

"A sugar momma who's into super studs? Ni-i-ice." Nick separated the pre-sliced bagel and loaded the halves into the toaster. "Is that how you're really paying for law school?"

Steve shook his head. "I don't blame her one bit for not wanting to meet my friends. I hang with idiots."

His phone rang, and he prayed Meadowfield hadn't learned his new phone number. But a check of the caller ID showed it was Qiang. He thumbed the answer icon.

"Hey, you should be at work."

"I am at work," she snapped. Her voice abruptly gentled. "Are you okay? The story was on every damn channel this morning."

"I'm fine. So is the girl I rescued. Thanks for asking." He couldn't stop the irritated burr in his voice as he realized why he was so upset. No one gave a rat's ass about Mariah's wellbeing. Not the reporters. Not the law school classmates who doxxed him. Not even his friends and family.

"Honey, it's no different than being a doctor or a lawyer," she said. "If you don't put some distance between yourself and the people you're trying to help, you'll burn out from the job. Then, you're of no use to anyone, especially yourself."

"Is that the real reason you put up your wall of irritation?" he teased.

"Yes." Qiang chuckled. "Harri does it, too, but you made me realize I was shutting myself off from my son and parents as well as everyone else. That's not what I wanted. Is she a friend of yours?"

"Who?"

"The girl you saved last night?" There was an odd tone in Qiang's voice.

"Are you jealous?"

"No," she snapped. "I am not jealous."

Steve decided it was safer for him not to pursue the question, though he got a little thrill from Qiang's defensive statement. "She's in several of the same classes as me, but last night was the first time I really talked to her. Her parents were putting a lot of pressure on her to be the top of the class."

"Ugh," Qiang murmured. "Like the professors aren't putting enough pressure on all of you already."

"Tell me about it." He chuckled. "Anyway, Harri and Aisha have everyone on lockdown, except for Susan because she had court this morning."

Qiang sighed. "I know. Aisha already texted me to stay away."

"So that's the real reason for your call? You were told you can't see me?" Steve teased. For all of Qiang's rigidity towards life, she had a wild streak in private.

"I'll come see you tomorrow night after my in-laws pick up Connor," she taunted.

"That's . . . not a good idea right now." Steve had been looking forward to spending the holiday alone with Qiang while her son was at his grandparents. The three of them had an early celebration last week with Qiang's parents. Two holiday celebrations delighted Connor to no end. When he suggested Steve adopt him so his name could be Connor Connors, an odd look had appeared on Qiang's face. She brushed it off at the time, but he planned to ask her if adopting Connor was such a bad idea while she was a little more relaxed.

"Why not?" No accusation in her voice, just curiosity.

"Nick and Bethany are stuck here for the time being," he said. "They helped me with our classmate last night. Aisha's worried Meadowfield will harass them."

A derisive snort blasted through the speaker. "I'm assuming the Carter Swift who has oh-so-graciously been doing interviews is the same Carter from your study group."

"Yep."

"He could be accidentally struck by lightning," she grumbled.

"If that happens, you know who Aisha will blame," he shot back. "I don't need her to beat me over the head with pine trees again."

"Does she have a plan yet?" Qiang asked.

"She and Harri are working on it," he said.

"All right." Qiang sighed again. "Call me when it's safe for me to come over."

"I will," he said. "I love you."

"I love you, too."

Steve ended the call. Nick watched him with a smirk on his face.

"What?" Steve bit out.

"You've got it bad for her, man." Nick shoved a forkful of omelet into his mouth.

"And?"

Nick shrugged. "If I were banging someone as hot as Nix, I'd keep it quiet, too."

"Is that how you're going to play it?" Steve said. "Keeping naming superheroes of the female persuasion until you get a rise out of me?"

"Hey, if Ultramegaperson is your type, more power to you." Nick shrugged again. "I'm not kink-shaming anyone."

Steve rolled his eyes. "Have ever you met them? Or would you say something like that to their face?"

Nick set down his plate and held up his hands. "I'm sorry if you think I was insulting your friend. That wasn't my intent." He lowered his palms and deliberately changed the subject. "Is there any chance Ms. Winters or your sister-in-law will let me go to my apartment and get some clean clothes? We may have the same waist measurement, but your inseam is way longer than mine." He raised his left foot and the leg of the sweats dangled a few inches past his toes.

"I'm sure Bethany and Mariah would prefer their own clothes, too." Steve rose from the couch and carried his dirty dishes to the sink. "It may require a stealth mission to get in and out of the building without being seen—"

The intercom buzzed. Steve walked over to the unit by the front door and pressed the button to speak. "Yes?"

"Serena called," Tim said. "Doctor O'Brien has appointments set up for Mariah at Lakeside Hospital. Mariah would like you to accompany her."

"Sure." Steve glanced at Nick. "My guest has a request for his own clothes. For some reason, he has a problem wearing my underwear."

Nick shot him the bird.

Tim chuckled. "Bethany and Mariah had the same request. We'll put together a luggage retrieval plan once Mariah's done at the hospital."

"How am I getting her out of the Lechuza Building?" Steve ran a hand over his face. His friends weren't the only ones who needed a shower, a shave, and a change of clothes.

"The Celia Express," Tim said. "Claire is waiting for you in the alley. Mariah's with me."

"I'll be right down." Steve hit the off button for the intercom.

"The Celia Express?" Nick's left eyebrow rose. "This the same Celia person Rey mentioned last night?"

"Yeah." Steve went back to the couch and slipped on his sneakers. "As you pointed out last night, Black Falcon needs ways in and out of his home without the supervillains seeing him."

Nick shook his head. "Y'all are weird."

Steve smiled. "Every family is weird in their own way." He grabbed his wallet and keys. "And don't even think about trying to sneak out while I'm gone. I can guarantee Tim and our IT guy Arthur are watching all the cameras in the building."

"I promise I'll stay put." Nick held his right hand in the Super Rangers salute.

Steve shook his head as he left his apartment, though a little part of him hoped Nick would try to leave just so Steve could see the look on his face when a retired vigilante and a former supervillain stopped him.

CHAPTER 11

Once Harri was halfway through her cup of black coffee, she dialed the number for the president's office at Canyon Pointe University. No cinnamon syrup for her with this call. She needed plain high octane java to get through this mess. The phone rang once. Twice. Three times. Four. Five. When the president's executive assistant finally answered, he claimed the president was currently out of the office.

Of course, he was. Typical chickenshit behavior at CPU. It was why Aisha's dad had quit despite his tenure. Marvin couldn't stand the staff and professors' extreme political games.

"This is Harri Winters of the Law Offices of Winters and Franklin," she said coolly. "Tell your boss to get on the phone right now, or the lawsuit concerning the university's violation of my client's rights will be on his desk by noon."

The assistant stammered a few times before he said, "One moment."

Harri tapped her pen against the pad of paper in front of her as she listened to a metal rock song that had been turned into an insipid instrumental. It was probably some administrator's vain attempt to appear relevant to the current student body and their parents.

The line clicked, shutting off the godawful music. "This is Randall Knox, Canyon Pointe University's in-house counsel. You mentioned you represent a student here at the university."

"So that's how President Cooper is going to play this?" Harri said. "Well, fine, Mr. Knox. My client isn't happy the university released his current address to Channel 12 reporter Ted Meadowfield."

"Which student are we talking about, Ms. Winters?" Knox asked.

"Really? You're going to play stupid when it's all over every TV and radio station in the state?" she snapped.

"Ms. Winters, even when I discover the unauthorized person who released Mr. Connors information, assuming it is someone working for the university, I can't cork the bottle. Maybe if your client didn't fly unmasked with witnesses around, none of this would be a problem now."

Harri couldn't believe this was the stance the university was taking, but at least, Knox decided to forgo the pretend-he's-an-idiot act. "Are you telling me you'd rather have a dead student on your hands? My grandmother is rolling over in her grave right now."

Knox laughed. "You don't have your family fortune to threaten me or anyone else with, Ms. Winters."

"I don't need my family fortune, Mr. Knox," she said sweetly. "I have evidence of a state supreme court judge's grandson, who also happens to be a student at your lovely university threatening my client because he is a super. How is CPU promoting bigotry going to look to all those parents who pay their kids' tuition?"

"Those parents are going to be happy we promote an even playing field when it comes to supers who use their abilities to cheat their way through law school," Knox responded.

"Including the parents of the girl my client saved last night?"

Knox remained silent for a long time. "Do you know who she is?"

"Yes."

Again, several seconds of silence ticked by before he said, "And why haven't her parents called me?"

"I think we both know the answer to that question, Mr. Knox," Harri answered. It was a huge bluff on her part. If he called her on it, she'd have to consult with Mariah before she could take the next legal step on her behalf, and technically, the girl wasn't a client.

Yet.

CPU's in-house counsel muttered an obscenity. "What exactly do all of your clients want, Winters?"

"Well, Mr. Connors would like the name of the person who released his private information," Harri said. "He also wants the false accusations of cheating put to rest."

"If you get the name of the person who gave Meadowfield your client's address, you'll leave the university out of the lawsuit?"

Harri started tapping her pen again. "That depends. Are you going to throw some student who works part-time in the administrative office under the bus, or are you going to make it worth my time and my client's wallet?"

"Give me numbers for each of your clients, and I'll speak with the board."

The university's board of trustees. Not President Cooper. If that wasn't a huge hint of who told Ted about Steve's address, the only thing more damning would be President Cooper's signed confession.

"There's still the accusations of cheating to deal with, Mr. Knox," Harri said.

"The school will have to do a thorough investigation because of the multiple complaints, but if Mr. Connors only has flight and strength capabilities, I'm sure he'll be exonerated," he said.

"Will he? With the grandson of a state supreme court justice making the initial accusations?" she asked.

"How do you know who made the accusation?" Knox sounded thoroughly confused. And he kept giving her everything she needed for the potential lawsuit. Maybe it was time to throw him a hint of how deep this situation went.

"Carter Swift was stupid enough to call my client and lay out what he planned to do and why." Harri had to bite the inside of her cheek to keep from adding, "Nanny nanny boo boo."

"And you have proof?" Knox asked.

"Yes," she said.

Knox sighed. "May I have a copy of the recording?" When she hesitated, he added, "I need something to take to the board of trustees. My client is the university. Cooper will not get a copy to hand over to the press."

"All right." Harri leaned back in her office chair. "I'll have the recording couriered to you. And by you, I mean, my head of security will only place it in your hand, no one else's."

"Understood," Knox bit out. In a more reasonable voice, he asked, "How is the girl?"

Harri considered what to tell him that wouldn't breach any ethical duty if case the firm ended up representing Mariah. "We're making sure she's getting the care she needs."

"I need to tell the dean of the law school what's going on," Knox said.

"Do what you need to," she answered. "In the meantime, I'll get that recording to you. When can I expect a number from the board?"

Knox chuckled. "You do realize Hanukkah has started and Christmas is less than two weeks away?"

"You do know it's the twenty-first century and you can video conference now?"

"I'll see what I can do, Ms. Winters."

After ending the call, Harri reached for the TV remote. Not because she wanted to, but she needed to know how far Meadowfield would go with this. The TV blinked on, and the anchor's blow-dried, overly tanned face filled the big screen.

"I'm in front of the Lechuza Building on Sixth Street," he intoned. "Stephen Koji Connors is listed as living here in one of the upper story apartments. The first floor occupants are the Law Offices of Winters and Franklin, LLP, who represent the notorious supervillain and escaped felon Miss Purrception.

"I have repeatedly called the manager of the building, Miguel Esperanza, for a comment, only to be threatened by him."

Harri sunk lower in her chair. At least, Aisha and Susan weren't in her office, chanting, "We told you so." Representing Miss Purrception had been one of Harri's few misjudgments in her entire career.

But honestly, she'd done it for the supervillain's mother, the retired superhero Rue Liberty. The elderly lady wanted her family back together before she passed, a feeling Harri could totally understand.

Harri nibbled on her lower lip. She needed some unbiased advice. What would Grandma Harri have done in this situation?

She smiled to herself as the solution blossomed in her brain, and she reached for the phone.

CHAPTER 12

Later that afternoon, Aisha sat on one of the couches in her office and held Mariah's hand as the girl spoke on the phone with her parents about her medical condition. Steve perched on the second couch, his face drawn and the skin around his eyes and mouth pulled tight. The tests at the hospital had confirmed Serena's analysis of Mariah's condition, though they couldn't confirm the type of tumor without a biopsy.

"They want to talk to you." The girl handed her phone to Aisha and released her hand to grab some more tissues from the box on the coffee table.

"This is Aisha Franklin," she said into the receiver.

"I'm Keymah Pendleton." The woman on the other end sniffed. "My husband Deandre is here with me."

"It's a pleasure to meet you both," Aisha said. "I'm sorry it is under these conditions."

"Is it true?" Deandre said. "Our baby has cancer?"

Aisha recognized the heartbreak in his voice. The same agony had filled her when she discovered she lost a baby and an ovary to an ectopic pregnancy after multiple miscarriages.

"The doctors won't be absolutely certain until they remove the tumor." She sighed. "But whether it's malignant or benign, the mass is putting pressure on Mariah's brain. They feel it's in her best interests to do the surgery as soon as possible."

"I-I don't understand how our daughter knows you," Keymah said.

"She's a friend and a law school classmate of our firm's intern Steve Connors."

"The-the boy on the news who can fly?" Keymah said.

Damn. Mariah was from Louisiana. Steve's stunt was spreading faster than the proverbial wildfire. Aisha glanced at Steve who gave her a slight nod.

"Yes, ma'am," she admitted.

"We need the truth, Ms. Franklin," Deandre murmured. "Did Mariah jump?"

"No." Aisha glanced at Mariah. "But she's going to need your support to get through this surgery, and we have no idea of how long she'll need for her recovery."

"I want her to get a second opinion," Keymah blurted.

"That's up to Mariah," Aisha replied. "However, I can say Lakeside Hospital works in conjunction with the Canyon Pointe University Medical School. They can give MD Anderson, Johns Hopkins, and the Mayo Clinic a run for their money."

Mariah gestured for Aisha to return her phone. "Look, I'm going to stay in Canyon Pointe for the holidays. If I get the surgery before Christmas, there's a good chance I can return to school in January."

Aisha bit her tongue. The girl had totally unrealistic expectations. While she may eventually return to classes, there were no guarantees of how much rehab she would need or how long it would take.

"Who's going to take care of you after surgery?" Keymah said. "You said your roommates are leaving for winter break today. We don't have any family in Canyon Pointe."

Aisha wanted to smack Mariah's parents. If it were Mitch facing brain surgery, she'd be on the first plane to be by his side.

No, she'd fly directly to him if she could.

"My friend Bethany said she'd stay with me when I'm released." Mariah looked shyly at the man on the couch across from her. "And Steve said he'd keep me company in the hospital."

"If you're sure that's what you want, honey," Deandre said.

"It is," Mariah stated firmly.

"All right," Keymah said. "Call us when the surgery is scheduled."

"Bye." Mariah thumbed the control to end the call and wiped away her tears with the sleeve of the CPU Law sweatshirt she'd borrowed from Aisha this morning.

"They've got too much on their plates right now," the girl said before Aisha or Steve could say anything. "They don't need the burden of my problems."

"Is that you or the tumor talking?" Steve said.

Mariah's eyes widened. "You know nothing about my family."

"I know something about family." Steve slashed his hand through the air. "My adoptive parents would be on the first plane to Canyon Pointe if I needed them. I know my biological mother did everything she could to protect me. And I know my brother and my sister-in-law would drop everything if I was in trouble."

"Well, good for you," Mariah snapped.

Steve narrowed his eyes. Unlike Rey's slow burn, his temper resembled a flash fire. There and gone in an instant. But that fire burned.

"Since I'm not any help, I'll go back to my apartment." He stood and stalked out of Aisha's office. At least, he didn't slam her door and shatter it.

"Do you want to tell me what's going on?" Aisha asked softly.

"I have a brain tumor." Mariah slumped against the back of the couch.

"You know what I mean," Aisha prodded. "Are you angry at your parents for not coming to Canyon Pointe? Or are you pissed you have a crush on my brother-in-law, and he's taken?"

Mariah sighed, and she rolled her head to face Aisha. "All of the above actually." The girl groaned. "I was a psychology minor. I know part of this is the whole hero-worship when someone saves your life thing. Another part is facing my mortality when I'm only twenty-three. Then there's my parents. They—"

Mariah turned so she stared at the ceiling again. "My parents are dealing with my grandmother and her health issues, my sister Kiki who has CF, and our oldest sister Tricia who can't seem to stay off drugs for more than a week at a time."

She swiped at the single tear rolling down her cheek. "Knowing the clinical details doesn't make the emotions easier to handle."

"That is a lot to deal with," Aisha murmured. "But it doesn't mean your feelings aren't totally valid. It's doubly hard when you're the only one who has their act together and suddenly you need help."

"I don't even have any real friends." Mariah sniffed. "I've been so focused on my grades, on my goals, I've ignored some of the more important aspects of life." She looked at Aisha again. "I've never even been in love."

Her heart ached for the girl. In some ways, Mariah sounded like Harri. Was that the real reason Harri married Eddie? She was afraid of being alone, but not in love with him? Aisha wasn't sure who to feel sorrier for.

"Why don't you and Bethany both stay here?" she said. "Bethany can't do everything by herself, and if there's a problem, you both will have someone nearby."

"You mean 'cause Serena lives down on the corner?" Mariah said.

Aisha chuckled. "I was thinking more that we have an unoccupied apartment on the third floor. With other families living in the building, someone will be here to help most of the time."

"I don't have the money to pay you—"

"This isn't about money." Aisha waved her right hand nonchalantly. "This is about giving someone who needs a break a quiet place to recover."

"Thank you, Ms. Franklin."

"My pleasure." Aisha raised her fist, and Mariah gently bumped it with her own fist.

A shy smile crossed the girl's face. "I don't suppose I could wrangle a work in exchange for room and board like Steve has here."

"Let's get you healthy first," Aisha said. "Then we'll discuss future possibilities."

CHAPTER 13

Steve tried to rein in his temper as he climbed the stairs to the third floor. Why the hell was Mariah taking her bad mood out on him? Between her and Carter, he felt like more of a punching bag than he did when he sparred with Aisha and Rey.

Shouting came from inside his apartment. He tapped in the code for his door and opened it. Inside, Bethany and Nick sat on the couch with Javier playing Foxstar.

"Javier! What the hell are you doing down here?" Steve stared at the teenager. "Why aren't you in school?"

The kid paused the game they were playing. "Dad, called me in sick due to the numerous trucks and reporters at our front door because of your stunt last night. He didn't want me trapped by those bozos."

Steve folded his arms over his chest. "Did you get your teachers' e-mails about your lessons?"

"Probably." Javier twitched and refused to look at him.

"You know your dad's rules," Steve said. "School work before video games."

"But it's the next to the last week of classes." Javier's voice cracked with his whine. "It's all busy work."

"Get your work done and turned in." Steve was finding it harder to keep a straight face at the teen's dejected expression. "When it's done, you can come back down here for pizza and gaming. And I will have Arthur check to make sure you got your homework done before you can play."

Javier practically leapt off the couch. "See you guys in a little while." He charged out the door and slammed it behind him.

Nick laughed. "Damn, you've got the sitcom father act down."

Steve shook his head. "Don't tell me you didn't pull that kind of crap when you were his age." He headed for the fridge.

"*Moi?*" Nick said.

"*Vous,*" Steve replied as he pulled out a sparkling water.

"How'd things go with Mariah's appointments?" Bethany set her controller on the coffee table.

Steve sat on a stool by the island. "Confirmed most of what Serena said. The neurologist couldn't detect whether it was cancer without a biopsy, but the tumor is pushing against her brain." He twisted off the cap. "It's probably the real reason she did so poorly on her finals. She knew the material."

Nick groaned and leaned against the back of the couch. "I wish I had that kind of excuse."

"Really? You want a potentially deadly medical issue to cop out on your grades?" Bethany shot him a dirty look before she turned back to Steve. "Has she scheduled her surgery?"

"She wanted to talk to her parents before she confirmed a date." His anger had sizzled out just talking to Nick and Bethany. "She's really scared, so if she gets a little pissy with you guys, that's why. Don't take it personally."

Which was exactly what he had been doing. No wonder Qiang questioned dating him when he was acting like a child.

"Poor thing." Bethany shook her head. "She's pleasant enough to be around, but I never saw her hanging with anyone up on the patio."

Steve bit his tongue to keep from repeating what was supposed to be a private conversation between Mariah and her parents. Just because he and Aisha could hear every damn word didn't mean their discussion was for public consumption.

However, Mariah's description of her parents last night didn't do them any justice. He couldn't imagine something happening to Connor and not being at his and Qiang's side as they dealt with the situation.

Together.

A soft knock on his door drew Steve out of his maudlin thoughts. He rose and answered the door. To his surprise, Mariah stood in the hallway, her hands shoved in the center pocket of the CPU Law sweatshirt she wore.

"I wanted to apologize," she murmured. "What I said to you downstairs wasn't appropriate, especially since you've been nothing but kind to me. I'm really sorry for acting like a jerk."

"We're cool. You're due a little temper tantrum after the twenty-four hours you've had." He stepped back and inclined his head. "Come on in. We're going to order pizza once Javier gets his homework done."

She entered and he closed the door. "Also, I wanted to say thanks to all of you for your help last night. I appreciate it, even if I didn't deserve it."

"First of all, you have got to stop feeling sorry for yourself." Nick jumped to his feet and brushed past Steve. He retrieved a cola from the fridge and handed it to Mariah. "Everyone has a bad day once and a while." He waved his hands. "Granted, yours was a doozy."

"'Doozy'?" Bethany laughed. "You sound like my grandmother."

"And my grandmother didn't like us swearing in her house," Nick shot back.

"You equate me with your grandmother?" Mariah cocked her head. "If that's the case, it's a good thing you don't have telepathy. Your grandmother would definitely be unhappy with the words going through my brain over the last eighteen hours."

"What are we going to do about our clothing and toiletries for tonight?" Bethany asked. "Does your friend Tim have a plan for us getting our stuff tonight?"

"Yeah," Nick added. "I'm on the tail-end of wearing my current contacts."

"And I can't be skipping my birth control pills," Bethany said.

Mariah looked at Steve with a forlorn expression. "I'd like get some of my stuff before my surgery next week."

He frowned. "You're not going to get a second opinion?"

Her wan smile said how much she was worried. "That's what today's appointment with the neurologist was. Unless you want to tell me your friend Serena is a fake?"

"I'm sorry." He shook his head. "I wish I could."

She turned to face Bethany. "Is the offer to stay with me when I get out of the hospital still open?"

"Of course," Bethany said.

Mariah nodded. "Ms. Franklin has offered to let us stay in the apartment next to this one. It's completed, but a little dusty, so once we get some extra clothes, would you mind helping me clean it?"

"We can all help," Nick said.

"Says the guy who left his towel on the floor of my bathroom," Steve teased.

Nick flipped the bird at him again.

Bethany grinned. "I wonder if she'd give us the same deal she gave Steve."

"I asked her." Mariah giggled. "She said we'd discuss it once I was healthy enough to work."

"Whoa!" Steve held up his hands. "Are you two running game on my family?"

"No," Bethany said. "We're exploring potential career options."

"Not to mention they have an awesome set of clients," Mariah said.

Nick glared at Steve. "You are dating Nix!"

Steve rubbed his forehead. "No, I am not. If you don't believe me, you can go downstairs to the daycare and ask her. When she shatters every bone in your body with her hypersonic voice, I can say I told you so."

"Nix is here?" Mariah and Bethany screeched at the same time. They looked at each other and darted for the apartment door, Nick on their heels.

Dammit. Aisha was definitely going to kick his ass for not being able to keep his mouth shut.

CHAPTER 14

Harri sat patiently in the atrium of the downtown office of Riggs Consolidated. Getting out of the Lechuza Building's garage hadn't been as bad for her with Cobblestone keeping the reporter and their vehicles and equipment out of the garage and clear of the exit.

Susan had already called to say she was spending the night in a hotel. She couldn't be late for a second day at Amperage's trial. But it was better for Susan to handle the nuisance suit. Harri's lack of patience would lead to calling the plaintiffs and their attorneys all kinds of impolite names. The idiots were in more danger from the high-voltage towers they built their neighborhood under than a superhero who kept power going to the city's grid after the Siblinghood of Bad Guys sabotaged the turbines at the Del Oro power plant.

"Ms. Winters?" Rigg's pretty young assistant smiled. "Boss Riley will see you now."

Boss Riley. Harri resisted the urge to role her eyes. Riggs was full of crap, and everyone in the city knew it. But to enact her plan, she needed to get inside his office first.

She followed the assistant into Riley Riggs' plush corner office. It was larger and much nicer than Howard Dewey's digs had been. The place was something the senior partner of their former rival form aspired to and never obtained. In fact, it reminded her of Grandma Harri's office in the downtown Winters Department Store.

Riley rose from his huge leather office chair. He carried his smile in his eyes because his huge bushy moustache covered a good expanse of his mouth.

"Harri!" His large palm swallowed hers, but he wasn't one of those men who tried to crush a lady's hand. "It's been a coon's age."

"It has been a while, Riley." She smiled and shook his hand firmly. "I've been rather busy the last couple of years."

He snorted and gestured for her to take a seat. "I told Al he needed to hire you back. The new guy in the city attorney's office is worthless."

"The mayor did send someone to feel me out, but I'm enjoying being my own boss," she said.

"And causing a ruckus." Riley commented.

"Is that the reason you had Mark hire one of my partners as your legal commentator?" Harri teased.

"I wish it were my idea, little girl." Riley laughed. "Mark and Nella put together the numbers. Franklin has a damn high Q score."

Harri raised her right eyebrow. "And it had nothing to do with Howard Dewey getting grabby?"

"Darlin', you already took down that nasty sonovabitch." His good humor fled from his eyes. "Is that why you're here? I'm next on your list?"

"No, but I need your help to stop your son-in-law from destroying his career."

"This is about the kid caught on camera last night?"

Harri nodded. "The president of Canyon Pointe University violated the kid's right to privacy by giving Ted the kid's address."

"So you're going after Cooper." Riley's statement sounded more like wishful thinking instead of a question.

"And Justice Swift's grandson Carter." She waited to see which way Riley would jump. He was one of Channing Swift's major donors, and there had been talk of Channing looking at a run for office in D.C.

Riley eyed her for a long time before he shook his head. "What do you and your boy want?"

Harri shrugged. "Replace one story for another." She set a flashdrive with a copy of Steve and Carter's conversation on the dark wooden surface of Riley's desk.

He looked at the drive and back at her. "Who else has a copy?"

"Other than me, Randall Knox, chief legal counsel at CPU."

Riley drummed his fingers on the table.

Harri leaned forward. "Our families have known each other for a long time. I'm asking for a favor for a couple of kids who didn't do a damn thing to hurt anyone else."

"There's a second kid involved?"

"The girl my intern rescued." Harri sighed. "No one gives a rat's ass about her, but if this circus continues, her name's going to come out. The last thing she needs are cameras in her face."

"Your intern might have done everyone a favor by letting her hit the pavement," Riley grumbled.

"You don't mean that," Harri chided.

"How bad is it?" He waved at the flashdrive.

"Terroristic threats against a non-costumed super. Minimum of twenty years in the federal pen."

"You could've run with this, little girl."

Harri shrugged again. "This incident and its aftermath could ruin a lot of people's lives if I took that route, Riley. I didn't go after Seismic Shift until he tried to kill the people I care about. Same thing with our previous mayor and DA, not to mention Corvus."

"I hope you aren't getting too big for your britches, Harriet Mathilda." The glint in his eyes said the hated full name was a deliberate attempt to get a rise out of her.

Except she couldn't afford to take the bait.

She stood. "I hoped you would see the casualties aren't worth the war."

"Hold on." Riley held up his hands. "I'll see what I can do."

"Thank you—"

"Don't thank me, Harri." He scowled at her, or she thought he did. "I'm going to collect on this favor some day."

"I know." She held out her palm. "Thanks for hearing me out. Call me when you have an answer."

He shook her hand.

As she left, she wondered if she hadn't just made a deal with the devil himself.

CHAPTER 15

From behind her desk, Aisha stared at Harri. "You would have been better off making a deal with Satan! What the hell were you thinking by trying to blackmail Riley Riggs? Or was your real plan to get me fired from the TV station?"

"You're leaving for Paris in a few weeks." Harri waved her hand. "You're not going to be working at Action 12! for a year."

"One, I'm under contract," Aisha spat. "And two, it's the twenty-first century! I can record my segment in France and send it to the U.S. where Nella can air it. That's what we planned to do."

"Look, I was trying to settle this quietly." Harri twiddled her thumbs instead of yelling. "No one needs their reputation ruined, especially Steve."

Her statement sent a wave of guilt through Aisha. Tim may have come up with the plan to send Black Falcon and Steve dressed as the Ghost Owl to retrieve the other students' personal effects, but she had seconded the idea. Steve hadn't been happy, but if his friend Nick had already put together that Rey was Black Falcon, she wanted to keep Nick guessing about which one of them was the Ghost Owl. Though in truth, Nick had probably figured that out, too, after she floated in Harri's loft last night.

"You're right." Aisha leaned her elbows on her desk and propped her chin on her fists. "But I'm terrified Ted's going to out all of us just because of what you had Rey do to his Corvette."

"For the record, that stunt was Rey and Arthur's idea, not mine." Harri slumped on her chair. "Things were so easy and innocent back then."

"That was less than two years ago, girl." Aisha laughed.

"Are you telling me our lives haven't changed a ton?" Harri said. "Especially with you leaving soon?"

"No, I'm not." Aisha sighed. "You're not going to start on me about Paris again. We paid Rey's tuition already."

"No, actually, I wanted to talk to you about something else." Harri cleared her throat. "What do you think about all of us going to Las Vegas for New Years' Eve?"

Aisha cocked her head. "Have you been smoking weed? We've already got a ton of work. Not to mention—"

"I meant for mine and Tim's wedding."

Aisha's jaw dropped open, and it took her a couple of tries before she shrieked, "Hell, yes!" She jumped up and raced around her desk to pull Harri upright into a bear hug. "Ohmigod! Why didn't you tell me?"

"Uh, Aisha, I don't mind the hug, but I'm going to upchuck if you continue flying me around your office."

She glanced down at the floor. Yep, they were a yard above the carpet. Thank goodness, there were high ceilings in this building. "Whoops! Sorry." She landed and set Harri carefully on her feet.

"It's okay." A rueful smile crossed Harri's face. "I want you and Rey at our wedding, and it made sense to do it before you left for France, instead of waiting until you came back."

"Wait, this was your idea?"

Harri's smile shifted to a scowl. "Don't act so shocked."

"It just means I lost the building pool." Aisha grinned.

"Building pool?" The tips of Harri's ears turned bright pink. "What were you betting on?"

"How long you would postpone your wedding." Aisha shook her head. "No offense, but you do have commitment issues."

Harri's eyes narrowed. "So who won?"

"Javier."

"Just for that I'm going to make him my flower boy," Harri grumbled.

CHAPTER 16

"This was not a good idea," Steve grumbled as he and Rey flew above the Canyon Pointe skyline toward the university. Tim's genius plan involved Steve and his brother borrowing the keys from their three guests and retrieving their belongings from their respective apartments.

In superhero togs.

"Why? Because you have to wear my former underwear in public?" Rey teased.

Jeremy had designed a Ghost Owl costume in Rey's size when Tim was trying to recruit Rey to replace him. Except Aisha had taken the moniker, and as a result, Steve found himself wearing the spare suit more times than he cared to admit while pretending to be his sister-in-law. At least, Rey was actually the superhero Black Falcon.

Steve sighed. "No, because acting like a hero is what got me into trouble to begin with." But a part of him was glad his twin wasn't chewing him out like Aisha had. And this was normal sibling teasing like Molly and Kerry exhibited. Maybe Rey was lightening up.

"No, what got you in trouble was rescuing someone without wearing the extra Ghost Owl underwear and a helmet." Rey chuckled.

"I'll try to remember that the next time a civilian is plummeting to their death," Steve said.

"Dude, no matter what shit Aisha and Harri give you, you couldn't let Mariah splatter all over the pavement," Rey said. "Anymore than I could have let all those people die in the City Hall fire. I just had the sense to grab something out of the trash to use as a mask."

"Point taken," Steve responded. He didn't feel like spatting with his brother tonight. "By the way, thank you for breakfast this morning."

"De nada." Static crackled through the comm before Rey added, "I'm sorry your plans with Qiang for the holidays got screwed up."

"Not totally screwed up, just delayed." Steve realized he was fooling himself. "I hope."

"It could be worse," Rey said. "Aunt Queenie could be coming out with Marvin and Betty for the holidays."

"She's not that bad," Steve said. Aisha's great-aunt had given him some excellent advice on how to win Qiang's heart last Christmas.

"Man, I actually had bruises on my ass from one dance with her at Martin and Renata's wedding," Rey complained.

Steve chuckled. "You know she was just doing it to get a rise out of Aisha."

"Maybe," Rey murmured. "She's not doing as well as she pretends."

Steve wasn't sure what to say. Queenie called him once a week since they'd met, and she'd sworn him to keep her secret. But it didn't seem right to hide her health from the rest of her family. But if Rey was willing to talk, maybe he'd have an idea on how to handle it.

"No, she's not," Steve murmured. "But she doesn't want to tell Marvin and the rest of the family the drugs aren't doing anything for her anymore. I know you and Aisha have a clue. You two can hear her breathing. I don't know what I should do."

"None of us are doing a damn thing." Rey's tone was gentle. "Queenie is capable of making her own decisions."

"But—"

"Everyone already knows. We're just going along because that's how she wants it." They flew past the Del Oro Bank building, the gold and red eagle ruling over the other city lights.

"What if this is her last Christmas?" Steve asked.

"Queenie won't be alone. She's spending the holiday with Renata and Martin because it's their first Christmas as newlyweds," Rey said. "And she can pinch the asses of Renata's brothers. It's a win-win for everyone." He paused before he added, "Or should Qiang be worried?"

"Jerk," Steve muttered.

"Schmuck," Rey replied.

They both laughed. For the first time, Steve believed things would be okay between them.

CHAPTER 17

Five days later, Harri peeked through her office blinds. They no longer needed Cobblestone to keep the garage entrance clear. Only three news trucks sat in front of the Lechuza Building this morning. Both Nick and Bethany had called their families and explained the situation. Surprisingly, neither set of parents made too much of a fuss about their kids staying in Canyon Pointe through the holidays, though Nick's grandmother should be nominated for a best actress award with the guilt trip she laid on him. She made both Betty and Aunt Queenie look as relaxed as a couple of stoners.

In fact, all four law students volunteered to clean all the tenants' apartments and lofts. Harri wanted to laugh at the sucking up act, but once they finished cleaning, Nick, Bethany, and Mariah asked to help with legal work. All three were as smart as Steve, and they dug into their respective tasks with a vengeance, even though poor Mariah had to take breaks. Apparently, she'd been suffering from severe headaches through the last part of the semester thanks to the tumor and hadn't told anyone.

Of course, the other three kids were all aiming for the same deal Steve had. Harri didn't blame them one bit. Plus, their assistance gave her the opportunity to make arrangements for the ceremony and to fly friends and family to Las Vegas over the New Year weekend for hers and Tim's wedding.

Harri sighed and let the slats fall back in place. Most of the media had jumped all over President Cooper leaving CPU at the end of the year. The only statement issued by the university was from the legal department. The press release, obviously written by Knox, claimed the board of trustees and Cooper had agreed to a mutual parting of the ways. However, that didn't stop the wild speculation.

What bothered her was not hearing back from Riley Riggs. Ted Meadowfield still ranted every night on the prime time broadcast that Captain Justice had faked his death and was now attending law school. To the point, commentators on other TV and radio channels speculated the Action 12! anchor was losing his mind.

Harri's intercom buzzed, and she strode back to her desk and tapped the button. "Yes?"

"Um, there's a guy claiming he's Justice Channing Swift on the phone for you," Patty said.

Harri hadn't expected a direct call from the judge. "Put him through, Patty."

She gingerly sat on her office chair. When the line 1 button flashed, she picked up her receiver and pressed the button. "This is Harri Winters."

"Ms. Winters, this is Channing Swift," the crisp baritone voice said. "I understand there's been an issue between my grandson Carter and your intern."

"Yes, sir." She knew better than to volunteer information.

"I'm in Canyon Pointe for an engagement," he said. "Carter and I would like to stop by this afternoon. He has something he needs to say to your boy."

"With all due respect, Your Honor, I think Carter said more than enough the last time he spoke to Steve," Harri said.

"Don't worry, Ms. Winters," Swift said lightly. "Carter's going to apologize to Steve before he heads to a rehab facility for substance abuse. But if you feel the need, I understand if some of your costumed clients are present to keep the peace."

"I don't think we'll need to go that far, sir. What time do you plan on being here?"

"Is two o'clock all right?"

"Two will be fine, Your Honor," she replied.

"Until then, Ms. Winters."

The signal went dead and she hung up the receiver. It was going to be an interesting day after all.

Harri ordered the other three law students upstairs before Justice Swift and his grandson arrived. She also asked Dajon to take Frisco and the babies up to the safe room in Miguel's apartment. The last thing she needed was a free-for-all in her office with the little kids in the crossfire.

Aisha suggested she should be present, but Harri didn't want Justice Swift feel like they were ganging up on him. However, she made sure Tim was the one to escort the Swifts into her office.

Harri and Steve stood when Tim knocked on the door and opened it. Once the justice and his grandson entered, Tim pushed the door closed and leaned against the wall.

Justice Swift stood about Tim's six-two, had a rather thick shock of silver hair, and wore a tailored dark gray suit with a burgundy tie and kerchief accents. Carter was the same height, his long blond hair was pulled into a bun, and he wore jeans and a Copperheads t-shirt. However, Carter could easily be his grandfather in fifty years, and vice versa.

"It's a pleasure to meet you, Justice Swift." Harri circled her desk and held out her palm.

The justice shook it and flashed a wry smile. "Just not in these circumstances."

"No, not this situation."

The justice turned to Steve and held out his hand. "Mr. Connors."

"Your Honor." Steve shook hands with Justice Swift.

"How's the girl you saved?" the justice asked.

"She's doing okay," Steve said.

"You did the right thing, son." Swift shook his head. "It's a shame a lot of other people can't see that."

"I've withdrawn my accusation that you cheated." Carter's jaw twitched before he added. "I'm sorry for how I treated you."

Harri's spine tingled. It was obvious the senior Swift had ordered the younger one to apologize, but it didn't sound one bit like he meant it.

"Do you think I should have let Mariah die?" Steve asked softly.

Carter's eyes widened, as if he hadn't considered that possibility.

"I'm not a psych major," Steve continued. "I was out of my depth. No one else at the party noticed her out on that ledge. If I left her to get help, I didn't know what she would do. So I stayed near her."

He sucked in a deep breath and released. "What should I have done differently to keep her alive and keep you as a friend? That's assuming we really were friends. Were we?"

The pain in Steve's voice was a palpable thing. There were times when Harri forgot how young he and Rey were.

The possibilities Steve posed were something Carter obviously hadn't considered before. He looked at the tips of his shoes for a long time before he raised his head and said, "I don't know. That's something I need to figure out while I'm in rehab. Can I give you a real answer when I get out?"

"Yeah." Steve nodded. "You have my number."

Carter nodded in return.

"Thank you for your time, Mr. Connors, Ms.Winters." Justice Swift indicated to his nephew it was time to go.

Tim escorted them out, but he made a point of closing Harri's office door behind him as he and the Swifts left. So he was worried about Steve, too.

"I guess I'd better get back to work," Steve mumbled.

"Sit down on the couch for a minute," Harri said.

"Look, I know I screwed up," he said bitterly. "Aisha made that very clear—"

"That's not what I was going to say." Harri pointed at the couch. "Sit."

She couldn't make him obey her, but something was going on. Something bad enough Qiang called her his morning as a neutral third party. And it was truly a problem if Qiang called her instead of Aisha. The superhero still held a grudge over Harri short-circuiting her powers when Seismic Shift had threatened Qiang's family if she didn't kill Harri.

But Steve lowered himself onto the cushions of the far couch. Harri strode over to her credenza and pulled out her emergency whiskey and two tumblers.

She sat on the couch next to Steve, set the glasses on her coffee table, and poured them both two fingers of whiskey.

"Aisha is taking out her fear for Mitch on you," Harri said as she handed one of the tumblers to Steve. "No you shouldn't have let Mariah plummet to her death. She's a good kid in a rough situation. And under normal circumstances, Aisha would have been the first one to tell you that."

"But we're not normal." A vague smile tilted the corners of his mouth. "Maybe I've been fooling myself this whole time. Thinking I could have regular job, and eventually a wife and family."

"You can have those," Harri murmured. "But you're going to have to work a little bit harder for it than most people. Situations like Mariah's are going to hit you when you least expect it."

He set his glass on the table. "Should I take some time off? Go to another school? Hope that this blows over?"

"Running away isn't going to make the issue go away." She took a sip of whiskey. "You are a super. You're going to take that with you wherever you go. You can still live up to your ideals without joining the underwear brigade. Besides, do you really want to leave Qiang and Connor behind?"

"No, I don't, but—" Steve picked up his glass and downed the whiskey in one gulp. "Connor wants me to adopt him, and I haven't had two seconds to really talk to Qiang about it."

"Wow," Harri murmured. "That's a load to deal with on top of everything else. Are you worried she's going to do something stupid like dump you?"

"I don't know." He set the glass on the coffee table. "Do you mind if I take the rest of the afternoon off?"

She smiled. "I think that's a good idea. What time would you like the reservations at Nolan's?"

"I think I'm going to pass on the restaurant tonight, but I may ask for a table in the near future."

"Don't go too fancy on the ring either," Harri teased. "Simple and elegant for her."

He chuckled. "I don't think we're quite ready for that step, but I'll keep it in mind." He hesitated for a fraction of a second before he added, "Would you and Tim be terribly upset if I didn't attend your wedding?"

"I didn't expect otherwise since you made your commitment to accompany Mariah through her surgery."

As Steve left her office, Harri found herself wondering what would have happened if Rey hadn't come to her rescue the day of the City Hall fire.

CHAPTER 18

At the knock on her office door, Aisha yelled, "Come in!"

Steve poked his head around the edge. "Do you have a minute?"

"That depends on whether you're bringing any teen angst with you." she said dryly.

"Paul giving you that hard of a time?" Steve stepped inside and closed the door.

"With Judge Inunza resigning from the bench in the wake of Carol's conviction, he and Paul are butting heads about the kid going to college."

"Paul didn't strike me as the type who wants the fame for the sake of fame," Steve said.

"He's not," Aisha leaned back in her chair. "He's concerned about his dad having enough to live on, even though the judge and Carol started saving for his college fund before he was born. I think it's hitting him that his mom's in prison for the next few Christmases."

She reached for her mug of peppermint mocha and gestured at one of her guest chairs. "Take a seat. What did you need to discuss?"

He took the proffered chair. "I want to apologize for what happened a few nights ago. I wasn't thinking, and I'm sorry I put Mitch in danger of being removed from yours and Rey's custody."

Damn, she was going to get all teary-eyed at his forlorn expression. She took a sip of her coffee and cleared her throat.

"Actually, I'm the one who owes you an apology. I overreacted the other night. You did the right thing by saving Mariah's life, and I'm sorry I chewed you out for it."

"What do I do now?" Steve waved his right hand. "My name's out there as a known super. Am I going to become a target? Can I even get a job—"

"Wait." At the tinge of panic, Aisha sat upright and set her mug on her warmer. "Are you planning on leaving us?"

"Don't get me wrong." Steve raised his palms, his fingers spread. "I appreciate everything you all have done for me. But I think I need to be a little more well-rounded. I'm thinking of taking an intern position in one of the courts. Nick, Bethany, and Mariah would all love to take my place here."

Aisha chuckled and relaxed a little bit. "Actually, Susan, Harri, and I have been discussing keeping all four of you. You have no idea how much billable work we've gotten done over the last week."

Steve cocked his head. "When were you going to tell them?"

"The official offer will be in their Christmas stockings." Aisha grinned.

"Are you going to take one of them with you to Paris?" Steve asked in a hopeful manner.

"No, you all need to get your degrees, which means staying here and finishing your classes." Aisha hesitated. "You are staying in Canyon Pointe, I hope?"

"That was my parents' suggestion." Steve shrugged. "They said they haven't gotten too much flack from reporters, but I don't know if they're telling me the truth."

"They are," Aisha assured him. "Tim and Arthur have been keeping an eye on them." She shook her head. "I feared that video of you and Mariah would go viral, but it only became a major news item here, and a medium news item in Seattle because you're considered a local man. Other than Ted's insanity and some speculation by some Seattle commentators about whether you would come home, don underwear, and go public as a superhero, it's been thankfully quiet."

She didn't want to add she suspected the NSB was killing stories about Steve. They wouldn't look real good either if it came out that Captain Justice was now Black Falcon. Such news didn't need to be added to the load already on her brother-in-law's shoulders.

"Does that mean I should send Steelrose, Bathsheba, and Doctor Ricketts thank you notes?" Steve asked.

Aisha laughed along with him. Steelrose's trial for attempted murder had drawn protests in Hermanville after her quick release from prison for bank robbery. With Hanukah in full swing and Christmas approaching, the battle in downtown Jerusalem between the Israeli superhero and the latest idiot supervillain had filled all the news media outlets.

"I thought you didn't want a target on your back," Aisha said.

"Point taken." The humor faded from Steve's face. "Are we okay then?"

She leaned her elbows on her desk. "What's really going on with you?"

He blew out a deep breath and raked his hands through his hair. They were exactly the same things Rey would do when he was unsure about something. Or someone.

"Things between me and Rey seem to be better lately, and part of me wonders if it's because you guys are leaving for France soon and he won't have to look at me for a year."

"I've noticed the change in his behavior, too." She smiled. "You've got to remember he's been alone most of his life. Me getting pregnant and you showing up at the same time was a lot for him to handle. He's finally settling into his new roles in life. If Professor Paranoia hadn't done a number on both of you, his acceptance of you would have probably gone a lot smoother."

"I suppose so." Steve gave her a small, gentle smile. "Thanks for being a sounding board."

"You're welcome."

Once Steve left, she stared at one of her Sarah Golish prints. She wasn't about to betray her husband's confidence. He'd expressed some misgivings at leaving for Paris in the middle of Steve's crisis. When she had asked Rey why, he said, "Because he's my brother."

It was good to see him warm up to Steve. No matter how crazy her siblings, both biological and foster, made her, she know her life would be much poorer without them.

CHAPTER 19

Steve lay on his side on his couch and watched the microwave's clock change to twelve a.m. It was officially Christmas. Dad snored and Mom's CPAP whirred in his bedroom. Nick didn't stir in the spare bedroom.

In the apartment over Steve's, Patty and Arthur were wrapping the last of Grace's presents. Next door to them, Susan and her dad spoke softly about her mom's dementia. Mr. Kennedy feared this may be Mrs. Kennedy's last holiday she'd be cognizant of.

Beyond Dad's snoring, Bethany and Mariah discussed her upcoming brain surgery over cups of hot chocolate and marshmallow fluff. Mariah was scared as shit, and Bethany did her best to soothe her.

He didn't blame Mariah for her fear. The idea of someone literally poking through his brain gave him the heebie-jeebies. However, he totally understood the eerie feeling of watching yourself do shit and having no control over anything. Part of him wondered if Mrs. Kennedy felt the same way. Were dementia patients aware of things, but they couldn't make their brain connections work correctly?

Steve rolled onto his back and tried to think of happier things. Qiang was coming to the Lechuza Building for the holiday dinner, and it would be the first time she met Mom and Dad. He'd tried to talk her into taking Connor up to Seattle for Thanksgiving, but she feared the craziness and unfamiliarity of his extended family would overload her son. Steve hadn't pushed. Learning the ins and outs of autism had been a major education.

When he told Qiang about Mariah wanting him to be there for her surgery, he'd been a little surprised she hadn't argued with him about it. This was supposed to be their two weeks together.

Damn, he hoped he hadn't screwed up things with Qiang over him outing himself. She was so careful about keeping her Sparx identity separate from her Qiang Reilly, CPA, identity. He didn't blame her for wanting to do everything she could to protect her son and parents. And Mother Tranh had made great strides over the last year recovering from her stroke. Qiang almost seemed disappointed her parents decided to remain in their assisted living apartment near the rehab center.

Screw it. Sleep wasn't coming anytime soon. He didn't want to wake his guests by watching TV here. He rose and folded his afghan before he headed downstairs to the offices. Maybe some of Susan's chamomile tea would relax him enough to doze off while he watched some inane late night show.

But when he reached the reception area, the lights were already on in the conference room. The dialogue from *It's a Wonderful Life* poured through the open door.

He crossed the atrium and looked into the conference room. A disheveled Rey was wrapping presents.

Or trying to. Torn wrapping paper and crumpled ribbons covered half the table. Boxes and shopping bags covered the other half.

"You okay?" Steve asked.

"What does it look like?" Rey grumbled.

"You look like a stressed-out new dad dealing with his son's first Christmas." Steve grinned. "On the other hand, you sound like Harri right before she tases someone. Would you like some help?"

Rey sagged in his chair. "Yes, please." He looked up at Steve, and dark rose flushed his cheeks. "I've never wrapped a present before."

"Pause the movie. I'll make us some hot chocolate so we can do this properly.

Three minutes later, Steve returned from the break room with two steaming mugs topped with marshmallow fluff. Since Patty kept the kitchenette stocked with it during December, he didn't feel too guilty about dipping into the gooey, delicious stuff.

"What about last year's presents?" Steve asked as he handed Rey one of the mugs. "Everything was so neatly wrapped."

"Aisha wrapped everything and shipped it to Atlanta before we flew out." Rey sipped his hot chocolate. "This December's been a little crazy between paperwork to live and attend school in France and packing."

"That I can understand." Steve set aside his mug and picked up the closest box. "How about we start with this one?" He eyed the label in Japanese. "A stone teapot? That's got to be for Susan."

"Yeah, Takashi found it for me." Rey scribbled on an adhesive name tag. "The pot and the cups are hand-carved."

"She's going to love it." Steve grinned. "Since it's a nice rectangular shape, let's start with this one. Pick out which paper you want to use."

"How did you learn how to wrap?" Rey asked as he handed over the roll of silver paper with candy canes.

"Grandparents on Mom's side." Steve stood and made room on the table to spread out the paper. "They had a card and gift shop in Japantown. They made a point of buying Great-great-grandpa Ichio's building he lost when the family was interned during World War II. Everyone in the family worked at the store one point or another." He picked up the scissors. "Now gently lift the edge so it's a little longer than the half of the box facing you."

Over the next two hours, they worked together to wrap presents. Rey bent the blades of two pairs of scissors before he got the hang of curling ribbons. But in the end, all the boxes were adequately covered so the recipients couldn't guess what was underneath the wrappings. The movie had given way to repeats of the old Rankin-Bass Christmas specials.

"Thanks for the help." Rey took a drink of his third mug of hot chocolate.

Steve looked at Rey and bit his tongue to keep from laughing at the line of white on his brother's moustache. "Dude, if you're going to keep the facial hair so you don't look so much like me, you might want to go lighter on the marshmallow fluff."

Rey wiped at the marshmallow on his face and licked the sugary substance from his fingers. "Guess I need to trim it in the morning. I don't need all of Christmas dinner stuck to my face."

"And you're welcome for the help."

"I hear you're not going to Vegas for Harri and Tim's wedding," Rey said tentatively.

Steve took a sip of his own hot chocolate before he answered. "I promised Mariah I would be there for her. The surgery got pushed back to Monday because the neurosurgeon wanted a finer detailed MRI after the seizure she had last Tuesday."

"I don't blame the surgeon," Rey said. "One mistake and someone dies."

Steve stiffened. "Do you think I made a mistake?"

"I wasn't implying anything about you," Rey said. "And like I said before, you couldn't just let her splatter on the pavement. Has my wife been giving you more of a hard time?"

"No, Aisha and I are fine." Steve rose and stretched. "I think I just need some sleep. Merry Christmas, Rey."

His twin lifted his mug in salute. "Merry Christmas, Steve."

Steve rinsed his mug and placed it in the dishwasher before he flew up the stair case. Maybe he needed to reconsider suiting up after all. If something else happened where he was forced to use his powers in public, he might as well profit from it rather than hide in his apartment. It was something to run by Qiang when she arrived at the Lechuza Building in a few hours.

Chapter 20

On Christmas morning, Steve couldn't sit still, so he shooed Mom away from the table, and he cleared the breakfast dishes. Once in the kitchen, he hand-washed them. Part of him was glad Nick went to hang out with Bethany and Mariah. He didn't know if he could hold onto his temper if his friend made wise-cracks about Qiang.

His friends' fawning over Molly last week had been bad enough. Thankfully, she took the hero worship in stride, though she nipped Nick's attempts to ask her out in the bud.

Just thinking about it though distracted Steve enough he bent the fork he was washing. He muttered an obscenity and tried to straighten out the utensil.

Dad lumbered over to the coffee pot on the counter to refill his and Mom's coffee cups. "Settle down, son. We've met your girlfriends before, and I promise not to pick my nose in front of this one either."

"This is . . . different," Steve murmured as he rinsed the fork.

"Why?" Mom perched herself on one of the stools on the other side of the island. "Thanks, honey," she murmured as she accepted the steaming cup from Dad. He sauntered over to the refrigerator to grab the French vanilla creamer she preferred.

Steve paused in scrubbing egg yolk from a plate. "I've just never liked anyone as much as Qiang before, and I want you to like her, too."

"Or is it because she's a super?" Mom had the same shrewd look when she was dealing with some complex aerodynamic math problem.

"How many times do I need to say I'm sorry for hiding my abilities from you?" Steve grumbled.

"We're actually bothered by the fact we didn't build a relationship where you felt you could trust us." Dad set the bottle of creamer next to Mom before he sat on the stool next to her.

"It wasn't you guys." Steve shook his head. "I was a kid, and I had a very irrational fear you would get rid of me if you found out I was different."

"Oh, honey." A very sad look crossed Mom's face. "You and your dad are the best things in my life. I would never give you up—"

"Xquic did," he said softly. "Getting to know her as an adult, I understand her reasoning. After hearing what Rey went through when his nurse was murdered, I understand Xquic's fears. Our father was assassinated by her family, and she was scared she couldn't keep us safe."

"But when you're a kid—" He rinsed the plate to give himself a chance to swallow the lump in his throat.

"Are you saying we shouldn't have told you about your adoption?" Dad said.

"No." Steve shook his head again. "That would have been worse." He smiled. "Not to mention rather obvious you were lying. But even though you know about me now, I want you to judge Qiang by the human being she is. Not by her powers."

"Steve, I hate to tell you this, but I've already judged her." Mom held up her hand when he opened his mouth to protest. "She's a single mother with a special needs child. She takes care of her elderly parents. Plus she works full-time as a CPA, and she's a superhero. This Qiang is freaking awesome, and I'm praying she doesn't think I'm a drag."

A knock on the door jolted Steve out of his shock. He'd never thought of Mom as insecure.

He quickly dried his hands before he walked around the island and gave her a huge hug. "Maybe I didn't show you and Dad enough that you're the best parents I could wish for."

Dad smiled behind his thick black glasses. He reached over and squeezed Steve's shoulder.

Another knock echoed through the apartment.

"Coming!" Steve crossed to the door and opened it.

"Hi." Qiang smiled shyly. She wore a red dress with black heels, but it was the Santa hat and packed red bag slung over her left shoulder that made her look damn adorable.

"Hey." He knew he was grinning like a fool, but he couldn't help himself.

"Can I come in?" she prompted.

"Yeah, definitely." He stepped back so she could enter. "Let me take your bag."

"No peeking," she said sternly as she hefted the bag off her shoulder, handed it to him, and stepped inside.

"Yes, ma'am." He took the bag before he made introductions. "Mom and Dad, this is Qiang Reilly. Qiang, these are my parents Tony and Jill Connors."

"A pleasure to meet you." Qiang held out her palm.

"If you're seeing Steve, you're family." Mom ignored Qiang's proffered hand and hugged her.

"Oh, um, okay." Qiang awkwardly returned the hug.

Dad snickered. "You're making the woman uncomfortable, Honey."

Mom release Qiang and stepped back. "I'm sorry. I didn't mean to do that. It's just Steve's been talking about you for nearly a year and—"

"Please ignore Jill." Dad shook Qiang's hand. "She's a little nervous about meeting you."

"Nervous about meeting me?" Qiang glanced at Steve before returning her attention to Mom. "You're an aeronautical engineer."

"And you're a CPA." Mom gestured wildly. "Half the people I personally know who've taken the CPA exam failed it, and three of them are attorneys."

"Thanks for the vote of confidence, Mom," Steve said dryly.

Her expression turned to one of shock. "Are you taking the CPA exam in addition to the bar?" Of course, she took his statement literally. It was the engineer in her.

"No, Mom, I'm not taking the CPA exam anytime in the future," he said gently.

"You could if you wanted to." Qiang turned back to his parents. "Did he tell you he earned the top rank in his class?"

"No, he did not." Dad regarded him with the same scrutiny as Mom had earlier. "He was more worried we'd do something to embarrass him in front of you. Like pulling out the naked baby pictures."

"Da-a-a-d." Steve gestured for him to stop with the teasing. He knew they meant well, but for the love of all that was holy, they needed to stop.

"I think I have a picture on my phone." Mom pulled her device out of the pocket of her slacks.

"You have a baby picture of me on your phone?" The urge to fly away hit Steve in the gut. She really wasn't going to show Qiang, was she?

"This was the day we got custody," Mom said softly as she held up the phone for Qiang to see.

Steve peered over Qiang's shoulder. It was the same picture that sat on Mom's home desk ever since he could remember. Dad held him wrapped in a Honduran, woven blanket in shades of red, yellow, and orange. He stared up at Dad who looked at him with such an expression of love and gratitude.

"It reminds me of the day Connor was born." There was a warmth in Qiang's voice, an emotion she rarely shared with anyone. "It made the thirty hours of labor worth it."

Mom chuckled. "That was one thing I was grateful to have missed."

Qiang's body stiffened against Steve's. "W-where did you get those earrings?"

Steve examined Mom's jewelry. They were the stylized Sparx lightning bolts from the accessory line Aisha had practically forced Qiang to license. The earrings hadn't even registered with him when Mom came out of his bedroom this morning because he'd been so nervous about Qiang meeting his parents.

"You like them?" Mom fingered the right one. "My mother and father own a gift shop in Seattle in what used to be Japantown. My sister Hannah now runs the day-to-day operations. She insisted they carry the Sparx's jewelry line last year. My parents were rather hesitant at first, so Hannah turned our other two sisters and me into walking advertisements."

"D-does your sister carry lots of superhero merchandise?" Qiang asked.

"She tries to stick to the more mainstream items she thinks would really sell even without the superhero name attached." Mom grinned. "Don't ever say this in front of Steve's grandparents, but the Redwood vibrator is Hannah's biggest seller. Pun intended."

Qiang nervously laughed along with Mom.

"Now that you've both embarrassed Steve thoroughly, would you like a cup of coffee, Qiang?" Dad said.

"Yes, please." She looked up at Steve with a mischievous glint in her eyes.

Yep, he was definitely going to pay for her socializing with the parents later.

Chapter 21

◆◦◆

Christmas afternoon in her loft, Harri gasped for breath from Betty's bear hug. "I'm so glad you want us to walk you down the aisle," her foster mother said.

"If you want to walk down the aisle with her, let the poor girl breathe, Betty," Marvin chided.

However, when Betty released Harri, he swept in for his own huge embrace. "Thank you for asking us."

"Even if it's an Elvis impersonator officiating?" Harri laughed.

"It's better than finding out one of your kids eloped," he said.

"Let it go, Marvin," Jeremy yelled from the kitchen where he and Leo were mixing drinks for everyone.

"You think we wouldn't have approved?" Marvin scowled at Jeremy. "We dang well knew you preferred boys when we took you in, young man."

"It's Christmas Day, gentlemen," Susan's mom barked from her seat on the rocking chair. "I won't have your arguing be one of the few things I can remember next year."

"Yes, Mrs. Kennedy," both Marvin and Jeremy said.

"Oh, dear! I need to get the gravy started." She started to get up.

"No, Mom, you don't have to do a thing this time." Susan laid her hand on her mother's arm. "Marta and Miguel insisted they make dinner since we cooked for them last year."

As if Susan conjured them, the antique elevator groaned to life.

"Harri, can you hold Mitch while we set up the buffet line in our kitchen?" Aisha asked.

"What? I can't hold my own grandbaby?" Betty stomped over to Aisha and carefully took Mitch into her arms.

"You need some help bringing stuff up?" Harri asked.

Aisha laughed. "No thanks. We've got an army inbound. I haven't had a chance to load the breakfast dishes into the washer so they've got room to lay out food trays."

"Honey, we need to wake up Mr. Tranh." Mrs. Kennedy looked at her husband. "He wanted to take a nap before dinner."

Qiang opened her mouth, but Harri caught her eye and shook her head. Qiang relaxed. If anyone here knew what the Kennedys were going through, it was her.

"It's okay, dear." Mr. Kennedy patted his wife's hand. "One of the kids went to wake him up."

"But Susan and Tracy are right here." Mrs. Kennedy had been calling Patty by her younger daughter's name since the Kennedys arrived.

"One of his own kids," Mr. Kennedy corrected.

"Oh, all right then." Mrs. Kennedy nodded. "You know he loves my turkey."

Aisha tilted her head, and Harri followed her into the hallway. When they were relatively alone, Aisha smiled. "Nella loved the Death by Chocolate gift basket, by the way."

Harri shrugged. "She could have made our lives miserable. And I owe you, too. I understand why you cultivate the press like you do."

"I'll make you a proper superhero agent yet." Aisha entered her own loft, leaving the door open.

The extra warmth from the guests hit Harri when she stepped into her own place. She also left the door open to get some air circulating. Harri walked over the island and held her glass out to Jeremy.

"You okay?" He took the tumbler and poured in diet cola.

"Yeah." She glanced over her shoulder. No one was paying attention to them besides Leo, but she lowered her voice anyway. "As much as I bitch about my mom and dad and stepmonster, I don't know if I could handle them with the grace Susan and Qiang do with their parents."

"It's amazing what love and acceptance can do for family harmony." Jeremy's smile wasn't his usual cocky grin. No, this one was tender and warm. "It's why we got along better with Betty and Marvin than we did our own folks."

"So if Elvis is officiating, is this a theme wedding?" Leo's eyes glinted with a certain devilish glee.

Harri rolled her eyes. "Tim wants to dress like a doctor, and he wants me to dress up like someone named Lake or Pond or something."

Jeremy cocked his head. "Did he say a doctor or *the* Doctor?"

"I don't know," Harri moaned.

"*The* Doctor," Arthur said as he sat down two glasses for refills. "No Daleks, Cybermen, or Zygons, you two."

"What about Missy?" Leo asked.

"I wanted to be Missy," Jeremy wailed.

"You could be Elizabeth II or Cleopatra." Leo grinned. "It's always fun when an ex-wife protests at the wedding."

"How about the mother of the bride?" Arthur suggested.

"Bite your tongue, boy!" Red flushed Jeremy's pale skin. "I am not going as a crazy ginger."

Harri walked away since she didn't understand a damn thing the guys were saying anyway. Down the hallway, the elevator rattled as it climbed the shaft. She hoped they hadn't over loaded the device. They didn't have enough to repair it after what she'd spent on the wedding.

She walked down to the gate. The rattling wasn't the elevator itself. The noise was caused by the four food catering carts Emilio, Reuben, Christina, and Rey had with them. Harri opened the outer gate and stepped out of their way.

"How much food did you guys bring?" she asked.

Reuben and Christina exchanged looks and laughed.

"We've seen you all eat, and we know how much you spend at the restaurant," Reuben said. "This is our thank you for being such good customers and hosting holidays for us."

Harri's stomach growled rather loudly at the incredible odors, which launched another round of laughter that even the rattling of the carts couldn't drown. Two more loads of carts travelled up to the fifth floor. The last load was the remaining members of the Esperanza and Hernandez clans.

Once everyone had plates piled with food, they gathered at the three tables they'd set up in Harri and Tim's loft, Miguel stood and tapped his knife against his wine goblet. Everyone quieted down, and he cleared his throat.

"Life has changed much for all of us compared to two Christmases ago," he said. "All for the better. I wanted a good life, a better life, for my sons than what I could provide. God has answered my prayers by giving us all of you. You have made our lives richer in ways that money never would. Gracias, and Feliz Navidad."

Everyone clinked glasses at Miguel's toast. Underneath the table, Tim's hand wrapped around Harri's free one and squeezed it.

Miguel was right. Life was damn near perfect, and she needed to appreciate it more.

"I love you," she whispered.

"I love you, too," Tim responded, and his kiss proved it.

CHAPTER 22

Darkness had fallen on Christmas night when Steve and Qiang climbed the stairwell to the roof for a little privacy. She wore one of his jackets and carried her bag over her shoulder. She had been passing out presents the entire day, including ones to Susan's, Aisha's, and his respective parents. However, with the weight at the bottom and the square edges, there was one more present inside the large red velvet sack.

A cool breeze caressed his face when he opened the door to the roof. The forecast was for snow flurries later in the week, but tonight was still relatively pleasant. He took her hand once she stepped past the doorjamb and led her to one of the benches Miguel had built over the summer.

"I'm sorry about Mom's jewelry," he said. "I didn't even notice—"

"Stop apologizing," she said before she gracefully sat down and laid the bag on her right. "I admit I jumped to the conclusion you'd told them about my alter ego. But your mom noticed my bracelet, so we had a nice talk about representation and how cool it was to see Asian-American ladies kick some ass."

"I didn't realize Aunt Hannah was carrying your line. I didn't go down to the shop the last time—"

She patted the wood on her left. "Would you please sit down and stop fretting about your parents, me, and the rest of your family? Everything went well."

"It's not just that," he admitted as he lowered himself to the bench.

Qiang frowned. "What's going on?"

"What would you think if I suited up?"

He had expected her to say he was crazy. However, she was so quiet for so long he wondered if he hadn't made a huge mistake.

Qiang finally said, "Are you considering doing this because of Mariah or because of me?"

"I'm worried about getting in the middle of another situation like Mariah's." The frustration jittered along his nerves. "I don't like hiding in my apartment for trying to do the right thing."

"What do you want me to say?" Qiang asked softly.

"I want you to tell me what you really think."

"If you decide to suit up, you need to do it for yourself, not because of what might happen or what other people, including me, may think."

"But should I?" he asked.

"Any answer I give you right now would be self-serving." A slight smile curved her mouth. "But you didn't want the double lifestyle before that damn holiday party, so don't do anything rash until Mariah recovers from her surgery. If you still feel the same way, then do it."

"Thanks." He hesitated about bringing up the other subject, but it needed to be addressed.

"Spit it out, Steve," she said.

"We need to talk about what happened with Connor."

She shuttered her emotion away, just as he feared she would when he broached the subject, but it had to be faced.

"I saw your expression during our private celebration when he said he wanted me to adopt him." Steve sucked in a deep breath. "Do you really think that would be such a bad thing?"

"My expression had nothing to do with you." She stared at her clasped hands on her lap. "It's my own guilt."

"Guilt?" He wanted to hold her, but he'd learn her moods well enough that if he touched her, she would quite literally fly away.

Qiang finally looked at him. "I've fallen in love with you, and I feel like I'm betraying Kevin."

Steve hadn't dared to say the L-word over the last year. But to hear her say it made him want to zoom through the sky, yelling at the top of his lungs. Except Qiang was a woman with stern expectations of herself and others. To fall for him and still love her dead husband had to be killing her.

"I'm not trying to replace him in either yours or Connor's lives," he said softly. "There's no way I can."

"I know." She exhaled wearily. "After you left our house that night, Connor came over and hugged me."

"He did?" Steve said. "That's great!" With Connor's autism, he was highly uncomfortable with physical displays of affection. His idea of closeness was sitting beside a person, but never touching them.

"Then he said, 'If I have enough room in my heart for two parents, you have enough room in your heart for two husbands.'" Qiang swallowed hard. "When I asked him what he meant, he said, 'You're sad, and Steve makes you happy. Daddy would want you to be happy, and Steve wants to make you happy. We can both love Steve. It doesn't mean we don't love Daddy.'"

"I love you," Steve murmured "And Connor, too. I've been afraid to say it because I worried you'd find an excuse to break up with me. It sounds like Connor has us both figured out."

Qiang shook her head. "I used to wonder how much of the world registers with him, but then he says something like that. He's smarter and less afraid than I am, that's for sure."

Steve feared to ask, but he needed to know where he stood with her. "So where does that leave you and me?"

She reached into her bag and pulled out a small square red box. "I wasn't sure about this until I talked to Connor. The stipulation is you have to wait until he gets back from Grandma and Grandpa Reilly's. He wants to be here if you accept."

Steve undid the ribbon and lifted the lid. Inside, nestled in white cotton lay a house key hanging from a bronze keyring with his name etched in the metal.

"Connor picked out the keyring," she said.

He looked up at her. "Are you suggesting what I think you're suggesting?"

She smiled. "Steve Connors, would you move in with me and my son?"

"Yes." He knew he was grinning like a fool again, and he didn't care. "Yes, I would, Qiang Reilly."

Steve replaced the lid of the box before he pulled Qiang onto his lap and sealed the deal with a very thorough kiss.

CHAPTER 23

Two days later, Steve and Bethany waited with a very bald Mariah in the pre-op area. She had decided to cut off her braids and shave her head before the surgery, claiming it was the one thing she could control. Leo had graciously let them use his and Jeremy's salon on Sunday, but he ended up taking over the job.

Nick had volunteered to stake out a spot in the surgical waiting room since the hospital would only allow two people to accompany Mariah from her hospital room to pre-op. However, he had a weird mix of disappointment and hope on his face when they separated at the elevator. It was becoming obvious he had more than a bit of a crush on Mariah.

Too bad Mariah was so consumed with the surgery she didn't see how Nick felt. Steve would have willingly traded places with Nick to avoid the bile that stung the back of his throat. Not from nerves, but the bitter chemical odor of hospital disinfectant. Sometimes, supersenses were a bitch to deal with in life despite what non-supers thought.

"Are you okay?" Mariah grasped his hand. Hers was warm and damp despite the frigid temperature in the pre-op area. "You look a little green."

"It's the antiseptic most hospitals use." He squeezed her unencumbered limb. The nurse had already started an IV in Mariah's other hand. "We're not good friends."

"Thanks for coming with me anyway." She smiled up at him before she turned to Bethany. "Both of you."

The nurse pushed back the curtain that gave them a semblance of privacy. "They're ready for you, Mariah." She and an orderly unlocked the wheels of Mariah's bed.

"Good luck," Steve said.

"We'll see you in a few hours." Bethany patted Mariah's shoulder.

Bethany and Steve stepped out of the way while the staff rolled the bed toward the double doors leading to the operating rooms.

An elderly woman dressed in the Purple Volunteers coat stepped closer. "Let me show you folks where you can wait."

It wasn't like they didn't know, but she was just doing her job. The hospital would need the bay for the next patient, and they definitely couldn't be running around the sterile operating rooms.

The Purple Volunteer Lady led them to the surgical waiting area. Nick sat on a couch opposite from another couple. "If you folks need anything, our desk is around the corner."

"Thank you," Bethany murmured.

"Now comes the hard part," Nick muttered as they sat down beside him.

"You sound like you've been through this before," Steve said.

"My grandfather." Nick sipped from the can of cola he held. "Mom, my aunts, and Grandma all fell apart when he had his heart attack. He was so old-school Grandma didn't even know where he kept his checkbook, much less ever used it. I was still in high school, but I had to take the lead in dealing with the doctors, insurance, and the hospital billing department.

"But the worst part of the whole situation was sitting in the waiting room for hours while they did open heart surgery on Grandpa."

"I'm sorry that you had to be the adult." Bethany reached over and hugged Nick. He patted her arm.

Steve leaned back and stretched out his legs. Might as well get comfortable. It was going to be a long day.

Steve woke up when Bethany prodded him in the ribs with her elbow. Qiang and Aisha stood in front of the couch with bags from Marta's.

He scrubbed his face. "How long was I out? What time is it?"

"It's about one in the afternoon." Qiang smirked.

"I don't know how you can deal with Steve and his snoring." Bethany stood and slid her phone into her pocket.

"I wasn't snoring," he said.

"Dude, you woke *me* up." Nick's grin was ruined by a wide yawn.

"Thank you for bringing us some food," Bethany chirped.

"Qiang, why don't you escort these guys to the open tables by the coffee shop?" Aisha handed Bethany the bags she carried. "I'll stay here in case anyone from surgery comes looking for them."

Steve stood and took the bags Qiang carried. Nick took the food Bethany held.

"No word yet, I take it," Qiang murmured as the quartet walked down the hallway.

"Nope," Steve answered. "The neurosurgeon said even with the MRI mapping, they could find a surprise or two. Right now, no news is good news."

"Did he say how long the surgery would take?" she asked.

"Eight to twelve hours, and that's assuming no complications."

"Mariah's a very strong young woman," Qiang murmured. "She'll pull through this."

Steve put his free arm around her shoulders. "Thanks for taking care of us."

"Ohmigod! Steve Connors is performing a PDA in public," Nick called out.

"Shush," Bethany hissed. "This is a hospital. Are you trying to get us thrown out?"

Steve laughed before he paused and made a point of kissing Qiang. To his surprise and delight, she didn't object at all.

CHAPTER 24

Mariah struggled to surface from the darkness. She blinked a few times to confirm she actually saw light. The room was strange. Not hers and Tricia's bedroom.

No, she hadn't lived at her parents since her freshman year in college. What year was she in now? Her head was fuzzy and achy at the same time. Law school exploded from the wool surrounding her thoughts. She was in her first year of law school.

A light shone from a partially closed door in front of her, and she could see part of a sink. Another much dimmer glow came from her right. Another door, but this one was closed. The light came from the space between the tile and the wood veneer.

Another glow on her left illuminated a person. She was Asian. Her dark hair partly covered her face. She wore a dark formal jacket and a light shell blouse. The glow was the screen of her phone.

"W-who—" Mariah's tongue didn't want to work, and her mouth was terribly dry. "Who-who—" Damn it! Why couldn't she make the rest of her question come out?

The woman looked up and smiled. "Who am I?"

Mariah started to nod, but the motion made her nauseated. "Yeah."

"I'm Qiang Reilly," the woman said. "Steve's girlfriend? We only met two days ago."

Steve. The hunky Hispanic guy with the gold eyes from her real property and Con law classes. They had been talking at a party.

"Steve—" Why was it so damn hard to talk?

"I made him and your friends Nick and Bethany go out to get a real meal." Qiang turned off her phone. "They were here when you came out of surgery."

"Li-li-li—"

"Do you want the light on?"

"Y-yes."

Qiang stood and reached for the switch behind Mariah's head. "I'm going to put this on the lowest setting, okay?"

Mariah squinted against the assault on her optic nerve. The motion pulled at her scalp. She reached for her head with her left hand. Lots of bandages and no hair.

Brain surgery. She had brain surgery. The doctor had warned her there may be some effects of removing the tumor. Apparently, talking had been one of them.

"Hey, don't be pressing too hard up there." Qiang gently but firmly grasped her wrist and brought it back down to the mattress. "You need that gray matter for law school."

Mariah's breath caught in her throat, and her heart threatened to hammer through her ribcage. She was such an idiot to think she could go back to law school. A sob forced its way out of her.

"Hey, it's okay." Qiang grasped Mariah's left hand in both of hers. "The surgery went really well. You probably don't remember the post-op tests, but you passed them all with flying colors. Your doctor thinks you'll make a complete recovery."

"Can-can-cancer," Mariah choked out between sobs.

"We'll know for sure in a couple of days." Qiang gently brushed Mariah's tears from her cheeks. Something, she couldn't remember Mom ever doing.

"And even if it is, you're a fighter, and you know Steve and I and all your friends will do whatever it takes to help." Qiang continued to hold Mariah's hand and caress her cheek while she cried silently.

How did she get so lucky to find these people? She'd been practically alone for so long. Maybe the holiday season really did produce miracles.

CHAPTER 25

◆—◆◆◆—◆

Three days later, Aisha slung three bags over her left shoulder. "I don't remember taking this much stuff with me the last time we went to Vegas."

Rey laughed while he buckled their son into his travel stroller. "Baby, the last time you went to Vegas was when you and Harri were both single. More than half of this stuff is Mitch's."

"But there's the costumes, too."

Rey straightened. "What's wrong with having a theme wedding? Or do you enjoy fluffy gowns too much to let them go?"

"Harri gets to wear jeans, a white-buttoned down shirt, normal boots, and a denim jacket," Aisha complained. She left out the part about the gun belt and the plastic orange replica of a six-shooter. It was some geek thing she didn't understand, and it wasn't worth the cognitive effort to try.

"What's wrong with us dressing as another married couple from the show?" Rey hoisted the diaper bag onto his shoulder and grabbed the handle of his hard shell suitcase.

"She gets to wear normal clothes." Aisha rolled open the door to their loft. "The tactical outfits we're wearing remind me too much of Corvus." She shuddered at the memory.

"Just remember we are the good guys," Rey chided as he pushed the stroller through the doorway. "Jones and Smith, freelance alien fighters."

"Jones and Smith? I could have dealt with a *Men in Black* suit." Aisha rolled the door shut and locked it. "Have you spoken with Steve today?"

"The tests came back," Rey said as they walked toward the elevator. "Mariah's tumor was cancer but with clear margins. Because of its size and where it was pressing on her brain, she's going to need some serious language rehab."

"That may be good news in a way. Harri can use that information against the law school so Mariah can retake her first semester classes and tests," Aisha murmured. "She may be a semester behind, but it would allow for an honest evaluation of her skills."

"You think she'll go back?" Rey asked.

"Qiang seemed convinced when she visited Mariah last night."

Rey shook his head. "Between you and Steve, Qiang's actually starting to act like a human being. Wasn't sure if that would ever happen."

"Be nice," Aisha chided as Rey opened the gates to their antique elevator. "She's covered our butts on more than one occasion."

"Don't get me wrong. I like Qiang." Rey pushed the stroller into the car, dragging the luggage behind him. "Her personality though can be . . . prickly at times."

Aisha enter the car and closed the gates before she poked the "Down" button. The elevator groaned to life and began its slow trek to the first floor. "There's a good chance she's going to be your sister-in-law some day. You need to watch what you say about her."

"I already am." A sly smile lit her husband's face. "I didn't tell him he was rushing into things when he announced he was moving in with her."

Aisha rolled her eyes. "If you did and Steve decked you for it, I'd be on his side."

"I have no room to talk, and I know it." Rey grabbed her ass, tugged her closer, and lavished a very intimate kiss on her. One that left her breathless when they parted and wishing they didn't have to catch a flight to Las Vegas.

As if he knew what she was thinking, he whispered, "I'll make up for it later tonight."

"You're damn right you will." She grinned up at him.

Little Mitch laughed and clapped his chubby hands at his parents' happiness.

Harri sat at the dressing table and stared at her reflection in the hotel room mirror. Jeremy had chopped off several inches of her hair. Corkscrew curls shot in all directions from her head. Leo had done her makeup. With the much darker shade of lipstick than she normally wore, she simply didn't look like herself. She looked—

Better.

So why was she upset about the change in hairstyle and makeup?

Jeremy placed his hands on her shoulders and looked at her reflection over her head. "Deep breaths, Harriet. You are not going to run. I'm not going to let you break Timmy's heart."

She did as she was told. Inhaled deeply and slowly released the air from her lungs. Again. Yet, it felt as if an elephant sat on her chest. Each successive breath became more difficult.

"Jaye?" Aisha's voice was questioning. She was in another chair by the drapes, her eyes closed while Leo applied her makeup.

"She's okay. Just pre-wedding jitters," Jeremy answered. He lowered his head until it was on the same level as hers. "Can you keep it together long enough for me to get my dress and wig on?"

Harri nodded. She didn't dare open her mouth. If she did, she'd vomit all over her wedding outfit. It was plain and strangely formal at the same time.

"All done, my Amazon princess." Leo's reflection bowed to Aisha's.

She opened her eyes, rose and carried her chair over to Harri. Aisha sat down, reached over and took Harri's left hand in both of hers.

"I know you're scared Harri, but Tim's not leaving you," Aisha whispered. "He wants to spend the rest of his life with you. He knows you so well he let you propose to him and pick the date. And he loves you very, very much. He'll do whatever it takes to make you happy."

"I-I know all that," Harri choked out. "I just wish my anxiety attack would get the memo."

"What do you want me to do to help you?" Aisha murmured.

"Hold my hand." Harri looked at her. "Don't let me run." A half-sob, half-hiccup erupted from her throat. "Don't let me ruin this. We'll be over if I do, and I can't lose him. Not with you going to Paris."

Aisha chuckled. "I knew you'd get a dig in on your wedding day. I'll be only an internet call away, sweetie."

"We're not going to be able to take a honeymoon right away." Harri stared at her reflection again. Nope, it still felt unreal. "What if we drop by for dinner one night while we're in France?"

"That would be great." Aisha gently squeezed Harri's fingers. "What made you change your mind?"

"Patty said she wasn't going to put up with my anxiety attacks when she and Arthur get married."

Aisha laughed. "He finally popped the question?"

"Not yet." Harri swallowed hard and turned to look at her best friend again. "But she's way more patient than I am."

That statement had Jeremy and Leo laughing as well as Aisha.

"Maybe there's hope for you yet." Aisha pulled Harri into a tight embrace.

"Don't kill the bride before the wedding." She tapped Aisha's upper arms. Sometimes, the girl forgot she had superstrength.

Aisha released Harri. "Sorry." She grabbed a tissue from the box on the dressing table and dabbed the tears threatening to streak concealer and blush down her cheeks. Checking herself in the mirror, she said, "That waterproof mascara is wonderful, Leo."

"Told you." His voice came from the depths of blinding white material he was struggling to put on.

"I thought you were going to be Missy," Aisha said.

"He asked me if he could be Donna." Harri waved her own tissue. Aisha was right. The mascara Leo had bought for each of their makeup bags hadn't so much as smudged. It was becoming easier to breathe, too.

"He's putting on a wedding dress," Aisha protested.

Harri shrugged. "One of us should be wearing a wedding dress tonight."

"B-But—" Aisha sputtered.

"It's canon for Leo's character, and he cleared it with both Tim and me," Harri stated. "And it's my wedding, so hush. Now, go help him find the armholes before he rips something."

A knock came from the main door.

"I got it," Harri said since both Jeremy and Leo were dressing. She checked the peephole before she opened the door.

Marvin and Betty stood there, grinning ear-to-ear. He wore a military dress uniform with a beret. She had on a skirt and blouse, covered by a lab coat and the same multi-colored, overlong, knit scarf Tim had brought with him.

"The guys have gone down to the chapel," Marvin said. "You kids ready?"

"Give us five minutes," Aisha called out.

Harri stepped out of the way so her foster parents could enter. Betty gasped when she caught sight of Leo. Aisha was pinning a veil to the red wig he wore.

"You can't wear a wedding dress when you're not the bride!" she screeched.

"It's okay," Harri said. "He has my and Tim's permission, and it's canon for his character."

"I don't care! It's not proper wedding etiquette!" Betty continued her monologue about the damn wedding dress while Jeremy and Leo finished getting ready, and she didn't stop during the long elevator ride down to the chapel.

Harri still feared she'd vomit. She and the Franklins started down the aisle to the Elvis impersonator singing "Can't Help Falling in Love." Behind him were floor-to-ceiling windows that overlooked the neon lights of the Strip. Harri's nausea eased. When her eyes met Tim's, the surety this was the right thing made her steps more confident.

He looked adorably dorky in the brown fedora, the long multi-colored scarf, and the burgundy coat. His face lit up, and she was sure she wore an equally ridiculous smile.

All of her friends, well, family, were dressed up in costumes. Some ridiculous, like Arthur as a sword-bearing lizard, and some not so much, like Patty's Victorian-era blouse and dress. They'd even dressed up Grace, though Harri wasn't sure why Patty and Arthur made Harri's goddaughter appear as a potato in a nineteenth-century butler suit.

But the biggest surprise for Harri wasn't Mitch's pin-striped suit and hightops, but the lack of facial hair on Rey. She shouldn't care about her law partner's husband on her own wedding day, but in a way, it relieved her. Maybe he was finally letting go of the illogical resentment he had toward his twin brother. As if to confirm her thoughts, he winked at her.

When they reached the dais, Marvin and Betty each kissed Harri on her cheeks before they retreated a few steps to complete the circle of loved ones. She took Tim's hand and squeezed it tight as they turned to face their Fake Elvis. He finished his song, and his assistant cut the music before he launched into the scripture about how love was patient and kind.

Tim bowed his head to hide his smile. She rather thought her requested selection would tickle him. All too quickly, the Elvis impersonator reached the part where he said, "Tim and Harri have chosen to recite their own vows."

Harri turned to face Tim. "Hello, Sweetie."

Her research paid off. A delighted expression appeared on her soon-to-be husband's face.

"Thank you for your patience and your kindness and everything else you've given me," she said. "Nothing I could give you would ever show how much you mean to me, but I'm going to try until the end of time."

"If I'd known the five-year-old kindergartener I babysat would turn into the woman you are today, I would have been a lot nicer to you." Tim grinned. "That little girl would have never stood by me through more surgeries than I care to count. But I want you by my side until the last sun winks out in the universe."

Harri turned to Aisha who pulled the simple gold band from one of the numerous pockets on her tactical pants. Miguel handed Tim a similar band that matched her engagement ring. They slipped the wedding rings onto each other's third finger on their left hands.

"By the power vested in me by the state of Nevada—"

"I've got you, Captain Justice!"

Harri whirled around to see Ted Meadowfield charge down the aisle of the small chapel with Bob the Cameraman in tow.

CHAPTER 27

"What the ever-loving fuck, Ted?" Harri roared. "You're ruining my wedding!"

"I got you for committing fraud, you two-bit con artist," he yelled back, but his focus was on Rey who held Mitch. "And I'm going to prove it on camera!"

Ted pulled a gun from his pocket and aimed it at Rey and her godson. Rey pivoted and knelt to shield Mitch.

Harri jumped between the gun and the Garcias. "Put the gun away, Ted, and walk out of this room now."

"Or what?" he sneered.

"I'll file charges for threatening my wedding guests." She tried to think, but the adrenaline rush from the very real danger blurred her mind and tightened her focus at the same time.

"I don't care." Ted aimed at Rey's unprotected back. "When the bullets bounce off him—"

Instinct grabbed Harri by the throat. She yanked the fake orange gun out of her holster and threw it at Ted. The heavy plastic hit him dead center in the forehead. His eyes rolled back, and he dropped to the chapel's plush carpet.

Bob ran down the aisle and kicked Ted's handgun away before he knelt and exchanged his portable camera for a cable in his equipment bag. A semi-conscious Ted was hogtied in ten seconds.

Aisha burst out laughing. "Junior Rodeo?"

"Junior Rodeo." Bob nodded. "Though I'm getting slow compared to my teens."

"Dammit, I would like to get through one freakin' month without someone aiming a gun at me," Harri growled.

"I'll call the police," Aisha said.

Someone cleared their voice behind Harri. She turned around. All the guys were pointing at Fake Elvis.

"I get paid by the hour regardless, darlin'," he said with Presley's trademark drawl. "But it's three minutes to midnight, and it's bad luck for the ceremony to end on the down stroke of the minute hand."

Cowering in the corner, Fake Elvis's assistant look totally flabbergasted.

"You got him, Bob?" Harri asked.

"I'll whack with my microphone if he wakes up," Bob responded.

"Keep an eye on the real and the fake guns," Aisha said. "Whatever you do, don't touch them."

"I won't," Bob promised.

"Two minutes, thirty seconds," Fake Elvis called out.

Harri grabbed Tim's hands. "State of Nevada . . . and go!"

"Inowpronounceyouhusbandandwifeyoumaykissthebride." Fake Elvis gasped for air.

Harri yanked Tim down to her by the collar of his burgundy coat and laid a big, wet kiss on him. Fake Elvis launched into an abbreviated version of "Burning Love." Harri and Tim parted as Fake Elvis swung his arm and crooned the last word.

The floor beneath their feet started to vibrate, and outside the huge floor-to-ceiling windows, fireworks could be seen coloring the midnight sky over Vegas.

Harri looked over her shoulder. "The matrons of honor can now call the police."

CHAPTER 28

❖✦❖

The fireworks had died long before law enforcement could get to the hotel where the wedding party were staying. Aisha coordinated with the police to question Harri and Tim first so they could have their wedding night in the bridal suite and Patty and Rey so they could put the kids to bed. To her surprise, Elvis turned out to be a Cook County sheriff's deputy. Performing weddings was his part-time job. The cops took his word as to the events more seriously than anyone else's.

"Ms. Franklin?" Bob sauntered over to her and Arthur. "I'm sorry, but the police confiscated my videocard."

She glanced at the police who were still questioning Mom and Dad. Everyone else's statements had been taken. She lowered her voice. "I know you, Bob. You have a copy, don't you?"

He lowered his voice as well. "This isn't Nella, Ms. Franklin. I'm under orders from Mr. Riggs himself because Ted's been obsessed with the idea Captain Justice is alive. I don't know what Mr. Riggs plans to do with the video."

Aisha smiled. "I've got a pretty good idea."

"If he airs the footage, it doesn't exactly make your husband look good." Bob's worried look tugged on her conscience.

"Bob, Rey did what he was supposed to," Aisha said. "Our deal is if we're ever in a situation where we're both at gunpoint, whoever has our son gets him clear while the other one distracts the gunman. I didn't expect Mitch's godmother to take out the assailant with a toy gun."

Bob chuckled. "Point taken. I just wanted to warn you." He shrugged. "I've already sent the video to Mr. Riggs, and he's wired a stipend into my account for babysitting Ted the last three weeks."

"You might as well have some fun while you're in Vegas," she said.

"Oh, I plan to spend every penny. See you at the station next week."

"Thanks for your assistance tonight." Aisha said.

Bob nodded and grabbed his equipment bag before he ambled out of the chapel.

"I can hack into the station's network and erase the video," Arthur murmured.

"You are not going to do a damn thing, Arthur Drallhickey, and that's a direct order."

"Why?" He looked confused, not put out, but then he considered Rey his best friend, and he'd do anything to protect her husband.

"Because Harri and Riggs made a deal," Aisha said. "The video gives all of us what we need to show Ted is crazy, and no one will believe his story about Steve now."

Arthur blinked. "Fascinating. I never would have considered that tactic."

Aisha laughed. "That only puts us lawyers one step above supervillainy."

The former supervillain nodded. "I've been convinced of that fact for a while."

The following Tuesday, Aisha did her last live in studio appearance at Action 12! The subject, of course, was the charges against Ted Meadowfield and what would happen to him. The atmosphere at the station was jubilant, to put it mildly.

But given Essie Morales's potential promotion to lead news anchor with Ted's breakdown, Nella assigned Kent Fairway to ask the questions on the legal analysis segment.

"The issue is self-explanatory from the video shot during the wedding," Aisha said. "He charged into my law partner's ceremony with a loaded gun, and he threatened to shoot my husband, claiming he was Captain Justice. Three weeks ago, he claimed our firm's intern was Captain Justice. Next, he'll probably claim our building manager is Captain Justice." She shook her head. "The only things the men have in common are their association with our law firm and they all happen to be Latinx, just like Captain Justice was."

"In the video we aired, it shows your husband cowering away from Meadowfield." Kent made the concerned journalist face, but Essie Morales was much better at it. "What was he doing?"

"Unfortunately, we were mugged at gunpoint when our son was four months old while we were out for an evening stroll." Aisha released a heavy sigh. "We made a deal after that. Whoever has the baby runs for shelter while the other one distracts the assailant. My husband happened to be the one holding our son since I was the matron of honor when Ted interrupted the wedding."

"What happens if Meadowfield pleads guilty by reason of insanity?" Kent said.

"The laws changed or were made more specific in the states and the federal criminal codes after John Hinckley, Jr., won his trial in the attempted assassination of then-president Ronald Reagan by pleading not guilty by reason of insanity. The State of Nevada uses the M'Naughton Rule to determine whether such a plea can be used."

Kent gracefully waved a hand at the central camera. "Can you explain the M'Naughton Rule to the audience?"

Aisha ticked off the points on the fingers of her left hand. "One, did the defendant know what he was doing? Two, did the defendant know what he was doing was wrong? The burden is on the defendant to show both criteria."

Kent smiled. "If you don't mind telling the audience, what does your husband do for a living?"

"He's in the restaurant business, worked his way from busboy up to chef." Aisha chuckled. "In fact, his dream is to study in Europe. This year, we're making that dream a reality. Any legal analysis from me will be coming from France for the next twelve months."

"Thank you and best wishes from all of us at Action 12! on the next exciting step in your family's lives." Kent turned to face the central camera. "Next up, Misha Winchester will be discussing tips on recycling those holiday leftovers."

When the overhead lights dimmed, Aisha spotted Riley Riggs standing in the back of the studio with Nella. He tilted his head, and indication for Aisha to join him.

"Aisha, seriously, good luck in Paris," Kent said as two of the techs helped them remove their microphones and battery packs. "You are coming back, right?"

"Yeah, definitely." Aisha chuckled. "My husband and a couple of friends have a plan for all of them to go to Le Cordon Bleu and then open their own place."

"I guess I'll talk to you in a couple of weeks when we set up the test video phone segment." Kent held out his hand.

She shook it. "Thanks."

They parted, and Aisha stepped off the stage and strode over to Riley and Nella.

"Interesting segment," Riley commented.

"Thank you," Aisha said evenly.

"It wasn't a compliment," Riley growled. "You know damn well my son-in-law is going to do time."

"That's up to a judge and jury in Nevada, not me."

Nella's head swung back and forth like she was watching a tennis match.

"You and your friends were the ones who filed charges," Riley accused.

"Riley, with all due respect, Harri tried to talk to you about Ted's behavior." Aisha glared at the station owner. "He treats everyone at the station like crap because he is your son-in-law. He gets away with it because he is your son-in-law. So when he started showing signs of aberrant behavior, everyone was afraid to say something to you."

She took a deep breath. "Including me. And because I didn't speak up, my husband and my son were almost killed over the weekend by a very sick man's delusions."

"I didn't mean—" Riley started, but Aisha held up a hand.

"If you feel the need to terminate my contract, there's no hard feelings, Riley," Aisha continued. "But I will no longer remain silent about things here in the news department."

A slight smile tilted the edges of his bushy moustache, and he looked at Nella. "Aren't you going to say you told me so?"

"I did tell you so," she answered dryly.

He turned back to Aisha. "I'm not breaking your contract. I am truly sorry Ted threatened your husband and your little baby. And I'll do everything in my power to keep Ted away from anyone associated with you and your firm." He shook his finger at her. "But tell Winters I'm not letting her off the hook. She still owes me."

"I'll remind her before I leave town," Aisha said.

Somehow though, her gut said she may be the one paying Riley's price, not Harri.

CHAPTER 29

A week later, Steve let Mariah hang onto his arm as he escorted her to her bathroom. She was still a bit wobbly on her legs, but she come a long way since the hospital released her. She also attacked her PT with a vengeance to get back on her feet. However, she still needed her wheelchair to travel further than the interior of her own apartment.

They reached the door of the bathroom. Mariah took a couple of careful steps before she could reach the safety bars Miguel helped Steve and Nick install in Mariah and Bethany's apartment before Mariah came home.

"Need some assistance," he asked.

"I got it." She practically slammed the door in his face. At least, she'd dropped the hero worshipping crap.

Steve shook his head and walked back to the kitchen where the four of them were arranging their schedules for the spring semester. Harri had agreed to Nick, Bethany, and Mariah interning with the firm for the next semester and living in the Lechuza Building as part of their compensation. She'd also negotiated with Canyon Pointe University for all four law students to receive credit for their internships.

Plus, Mariah was allowed to retake the 1L courses she failed without paying for them twice. It meant packing in a half semester's work over the next two summers, but Steve had faith she could do it.

Even better, the news story about his rescue of Mariah had faded over the past month. The other news organizations had dropped their pursuit of the matter when Ted Meadowfield's mental health issues became public.

Steve sat down at the table. "Is Mariah too much to handle?"

Bethany looked up at him. "Does Dajon know what he's getting into by watching Connor while you work during the afternoons?"

She had a point, but the firm's new daycare director seemed up to the challenge. Connor looked forward to spending time with Miguel's son Javier, though part of the conditions of Connor coming to the Lechuza Building after school was that he needed to do his homework before any videogaming.

"Tim has been a bear after each of his surgeries." Steve shrugged. "I don't know what we'll do if she pisses you off and you move out."

"I'm not going anywhere," Bethany stated. "Between the physical and psych therapies, all the docs seem certain her most of her depression was a side effect of the damn tumor. And she's the easiest roommate I've ever lived with."

"That makes me sound like a prostitute." Mariah said.

Steve tensed as she took halting steps across the kitchen, but he didn't want to embarrass her or piss her off by helping when she didn't ask for it. She reach her chair and dropped into it, but she winced.

"Charley horse?" Nick asked.

"Yeah," she murmured. "Both calves at the same time."

Nick scooted his chair beside hers and motioned for her to turn her chair. "Gimme."

"This is so weird." But Mariah shifted her chair. Nick gently pushed up the right leg of her sweatpants before his fingers dug into the cramping muscle.

"You need to be drinking more water before you go to PT," he gently chided.

"I do," she protested.

The alarm on Steve's phone chirped. "That's it for me. See you all tomorrow."

"Good night, Dad," Bethany teased.

Steve stood and slung on his jacket. "You kids get your homework done." He gathered his things and left to a chorus of good-byes.

Fifteen minutes later, he was in the pick-up lane at Connor's school. The teen jogged up to Steve's truck, his backpack bouncing to his strides. He climbed into the cab and slammed the door shut.

"Safety first," the kid muttered. He buckled his seatbelt before he nodded and stared straight ahead. "My body is secured."

"All right." Steve checked his mirrors and pulled into the exit lane. "How was school?"

"It was adequate." Connor hesitated. "Are you going to ask Mom to marry you?"

Steve smiled. "I'd like to. How would you feel about that?"

"You should speak with Grandfather first. He is very traditional." Another pause followed. "You should enlist my aid in picking out the ring after you speak with him."

"I planned on it."

"Excellent." Even though, Connor continued staring out the windshield, a ghost of a smile tilted the corner of his mouth. For him, that was high praise.

Steve smiled to himself. Yep, this was definitely going to be an excellent New Year.

CHAPTER 30

In his cell in the Las Vegas jail, Ted Meadowfield lay on his cot and stared at the ceiling. This place stunk to high heaven. Even worse, the judge refused to grant bail, claiming he was a flight risk. Riley could have fixed things. The fact Holland and his father-in-law left him here to rot pissed off Ted to no end.

He sat up when he heard voices in the corridor. A face peered into the cell before keys rattled in the lock. The guards shoved in a medium-sized man with dark shaggy hair and pasty skin. He wore the same orange jumpsuit Ted was forced to wear. The door slammed shut.

The new guy looked at Ted and started laughing. "You dye your skin to match your outfit?"

Recognition clicked in Ted's head. "Why'd they put someone like Gentleman Jared in the general population?"

The supervillain shrugged. "Ran out of space in the supers wing?"

"What would you want in order to teach me what you know?"

Gentleman Jared sniffed. "I don't do reporters."

"I'm not a reporter anymore." Ted lifted his chin. "And the only way to clear my name against the word of a bunch of superheroes is to become a supervillain."

Gentleman Jared smiled, showing his sharp, pointed teeth. "Maybe I could help. It's been a long time since I've tasted a superhero."

Harri and Tim are hitched. Aisha and Rey are on their way to Paris. Everything's going great, right? Nope, our heroes' aren't that lucky. Turn the page for a preview of *Hero Ad Litem*!

Bonus Excerpt
©2022, Suzan Harden

HERO AD LITEM

Harri Winters opened her eyes and rolled over on her back. Some wrongness had infiltrated her sleep. No, it was the absence of something.

She was in her own bed in her own bedroom from the greenish glow of her alarm clock. Her husband Tim lay beside her, snoring slightly. She inhaled deeply.

That was it. A lack of coffee aroma from the loft across the hall. Even though Rey didn't drink the beverage himself, he always got up early to make Aisha a pot of coffee.

Tim jerked upright. "What's wrong?"

Harri chuckled. "I never realized how much we depended on Rey to start our own days."

Tim groaned and flopped down on the mattress. "This is why we should get a coffee pot with a timer."

She cuddled against his side and pulled the covers over them both. "Can't you install a timer on our current coffee maker?"

"I could." He wrapped his arms around her and squeezed. "But it's kind of a waste of my talents considering coffee pots with timers are already on the market." He yawned.

"It's too quiet with them gone," she murmured.

"When does Aisha start back to work?"

"Today," Harri said. "I don't think it's her being gone that bothers me as much as missing some of our godson's milestones. Mitch will be walking by the time they return to the states."

"Let's just pray he's not flying yet when they get back," Tim said. "Regular parents do not realize how fast toddlers can be. If Mitch ends up with Rey and Aisha's power set, he'll be hell to deal with."

"Locks on the cookie jar?"

"I was thinking more of a titanium-reinforced safe for all the junk food."

Harri giggled at the idea. "You could probably sell that to a ton of parents."

"Heck, I could use one to keep you from eating all my Girl Scout cookies next month."

"I said I was sorry!"

"Prove it."

She rolled on top of him and proceeded in her very thorough apology.

Later that morning, Harri took her first sip from her second cup of coffee when the intercom buzzed. She glanced at the two clocks displayed on the corner of her laptop's monitor. Nine a.m. in Canyon Pointe equated to five p.m. in Paris. Aisha was right on time.

Harri jabbed the intercom button. "Yes?"

"Cathy Blanchett from the 126th Family Court is on line 1 for you," Patty chirped.

"Thanks. If Aisha calls while I'm on the phone with the court, tell her I'll call her back in a few minutes."

"Sure thing," Patty said.

Harri picked up the receiver and punched the flashing button. "Hey, Cathy, what can I do for you?"

"It's your turn to play ad litem," the court clerk replied.

"Already?" Harri sat back in her chair. "I just signed up in December." In fact her boyfriend and all her staff insisted she volunteer as an ad litem in the family courts. Apparently, they were all tired of her mothering them.

"The judge needs someone with supers experience, Harri." Cathy sighed. "The parents are in the middle of an ugly divorce, and she wants someone who will actually look out for the kid."

"Are the parents supers?" Harri sat up and flipped her legal pad to a clean page.

"Nope, but they're both looking at the kid as a meal ticket, which is why there's a huge battle for custody." Cathy paused a second before she added, "Harri, if you don't take custody of him, you know the NSB will. Special Agent Nesmith said they'd back off if you are assigned as ad litem. He was adamant no one else would do."

Special Agent Wilbur Nesmith had become a particular thorn in Harri's backside. He was doing his damnedest to earn the firm's trust. But someone within the National Superhero Bureau had set up Rey to be abducted and experimented on by Professor Paranoia, so trust of the NSB didn't come easy to anyone at Winters and Franklin.

And Harri knew she'd be lying to herself if she thought Rey, Aisha, and Mitch were totally safe from the U.S. government while they were in France.

"All right." She sighed. "I'm assuming you already made arrangements for me to meet with the kid?"

"The next hearing is scheduled for two this afternoon to decide who gets temporary custody," Cathy said.

"Nothing like waiting until the last minute," Harri grumbled. "How old is he?"

"Thirteen."

Line 2 started blinking on Harri's phone set.

"Cathy, can you shoot me a copy of the file by e-mail? I've got an international call scheduled for now."

"Sure thing," the court clerk chirped. "See you at two."

Harri clenched her teeth. If this kid's case didn't keep her mind off her godson, nothing else on earth would.

•141•

Want to check out a brand new series? Turn the page for a special preview of *Pestilence in Pumpkin Spice*, the first book in Soccer Moms of the Apocalypse!

Bonus Excerpt
©2022, Suzan Harden

PESTILENCE IN PUMPKIN SPICE

Penny Hudson guided her white minivan into one of the five free parking slots in the Oakfield Recreational Center lot while she tried to ignore the pain behind her eye sockets that had plagued her since lunchtime. The trees around the soccer fields had turned from green to gold and orange since last week's games. Brilliant leaves gleamed against the dark clouds to the west. The falling barometric pressure from the incoming weather front was probably the cause of her headache.

It would be a race between the soccer teams finishing the last round of games for Tuesday evening and the storm threatening to put an end to the park's activities. No sooner had she put the transmission into park, her daughter Justine yanked the back door of the vehicle open, jumped out, and raced up the sidewalk toward the park gate.

And left the dang van door wide open.

"Puberty, thou art a heartless bitch," Penny muttered under her breath. Their relationship had seemed to disintegrate when Justine turned twelve this summer. The last thing she needed was a major mother-daughter meltdown in front of the snooty parents and the resulting clucks and advice.

Francine Coy-Astin could be snooty, but she was the only stay-at-home team mom who would acknowledge the existence of the three working moms. Plus, Francine's daughter Brittany was a better player than most of the boys, which meant Francine was persona non grata with the rest of the moms for having an athletic daughter, so she hung out with the other three outcasts.

The crisp fall air and the scent of burning leaves mixed with the aromas of the four coffees in the drink carrier sitting on the front passenger seat. Children's shouts and cheers followed on the wind. Penny stabbed the button to close the back door. Thank goodness, she managed to talk Gene into the top package with the power doors when they bought the van. Otherwise, she might be tempted to slam the head of their only child in the manual doors of her old mini utility vehicle.

Penny tucked her purse under the driver seat and collected the drink carrier. With the chill wind and the overcast sky, she was glad she remembered to wear her sweatshirt. She pressed the locking button on her fob. The minivan beeped, its lights flashed, and she shoved the fob into her front jeans pocket.

A brand-new minivan, one she didn't recognize, was parked near the entrance to the stands. She felt a little sorry for the owner. Courtney Lasser, the president of the Oakfield Parents Association, and the rest of her stuck-up crew would definitely mock the puke green color. She started to pass it when she spotted the gold Saint Christopher medallion hanging from the rearview mirror.

And recognized the dark-haired woman with her head leaning against the steering wheel.

Penny walked around the van and knocked on the driver side window. Dani Elante jerked her head up and wildly looked around. Penny stepped back as her friend popped open the door.

"You okay?" Penny handed the Valencia double mocha from her coffee shop to Dani.

Her friend took a deep breath of the steam that wisped from her cup. "Yeah. Nothing military school wouldn't fix."

Penny rolled her eyes. "Puberty. God's punishment for one night of fun. If it makes you feel better, Justine began breakfast with the announcement that I needed to start buying her tampons."

Dani winced. "In front of Gene's dad?"

"Yep." Brown and yellow leaves crunched beneath their feet as they walked up the sidewalk to the entrance of the soccer field. They both paid the token fee to attend the game. Courtney's second in command Helen Chow made a point of glaring at their cups from Penny's coffee shop while she took their cash. Penny and Dani made an equal point of ignoring her. Cream, sugar, and a bottle of antacid couldn't redeem the burnt sludge served at the league's refreshment stand.

They started walking toward the aluminum torture devices the Oakfield Park Service referred to as audience stands. "I then got a lecture from Edward about how it would be my fault if Justine got knocked up before she graduated because I was too permissive with my hippy lifestyle."

"Maybe it's time to drop your bomb," Dani said.

Penny shook her head. "If he knew I knew he had an affair while Laura was in hospice, it would kill him."

"I'd do it," Dani said.

Penny chuckled. "No, you wouldn't. You are the last person in the world who would hurt someone."

"What is his problem with you?"

"According to him, I'm un-American for dressing up a plain cup of joe."

Dani laughed. "But you're the epitome of capitalism."

"Speaking of capitalism, I heard that developer Rimmon bought the Spenser Building downtown and plans to tear it down."

"Yeah, the Oakfield Historic Association is throwing a hissy fit, but that place is a death trap." Dani shook her head. "If the association really cared, they should have raised the funds to restore it before the roof caved in."

Penny climbed behind Dani to the top of the stands where Wila Ardale had claimed their usual spot, well away from the rest of the Tiger Shark team parents.

"I see you joined the minivan brigade." Wila's teeth flashed against her dark skin.

"I didn't have a choice," Dani grumbled.

Penny snorted as she handed Wila her white chocolate mocha. "Yes, you did. Chuck was being a cheap ass, and you should have called him on it."

Dani bristled at the criticism of her father. "It's a temporary vehicle until I can save up for another pickup."

Penny tilted her head. "His idea of temporary involved you working at the insurance company for just a year after you gave birth so you had experience on your resume."

Dani winced at that remark. "Marty needs the help."

Penny snorted a second time. "And every time you try to quit to finish your degree, your dad lays a million reasons on you not to leave, and your brother gives you a raise. When are you going to start living your own life?"

"I like working there." Dani's statement sounded half-hearted. "Besides you're the one saying I didn't do my fair share of carpooling, so a minivan makes sense."

"At least mine's not vomit green," Penny mumbled into her cup.

Wila leaned over and gave Dani a knowing wink. "Don't let her rattle your cage. She's just saying that because she keeps losing her minivan in the sea of white ones at the mall."

Penny scowled at Wila. "At least I don't need to make a spectacle of myself with that bright red atrocity you choose."

Dani sighed. "I miss my pickup."

"You're damn lucky that drunk driver didn't kill you. A truck can be replaced." Penny took another sip of her coffee. "But you and Mark can't." She immediately regretted her words at Dani's bleak expression. "I'm sorry. I shouldn't have—"

Dani waved her free hand and sniffed back the threatening tears. "It's not like I haven't been thinking the same thing. Wila can tell you what a mess I was at the scene."

"Actually, I was more worried Sergeant Park would end up arresting you for murder the way you were beating on the other driver." Wila peered over her shoulder at Dani's new minivan. "Let me guess. Chuck took the best deal on Neal's lot."

Penny appreciated Wila changing the subject. She'd first met Dani shortly after her husband Heath had been killed by another drunk driver. Dani had sat in Penny's café, staring blankly at the wall while her plain black coffee grew cold. The two women had bonded while Dani tried to put her life back together.

Francine plopped down next to Dani. "Neal told him he could order a pickup in whatever color you guys wanted." Her hot pink manicure contrasted with the olive green liquid in her reusable drink bottle. She must still be on her juicing cleanse.

Penny handed Francine her double French vanilla espresso. She popped off the lid of the coffee cup, unscrewed the cap on her bottle, and poured the espresso into the juice.

"Why can't you drink coffee like a normal person?" Penny shuddered in disgust.

Francine screwed the cap back on and shook her bottle to mix the contents. "Because I care about my health and my family's health." She took a drink of her noxious-looking mixture. "It's why none of my family caught that crud you brought back from your Florida vacation."

"Yeah." Penny rolled her eyes. "I specifically brought back the plague just to infect the entire town."

She sipped her pumpkin spice latte. The caffeine helped her headache, but the wind picked up, driving dead leaves across the field and sucking away the little warmth she got from the hot milk and espresso. The coaches gathered their teams for their pre-game huddle. Justine's face puckered into a pout when Coach Cordero named the starters who ran out to take their positions.

Justine stomped back to the bench and dropped on it dramatically. At least, the coach had called and discussed the fight between her daughter and Kenny Lasser. Cordero said he would have benched Justine for taunting Kenny at Thursday's practice regardless of any threats from Courtney. He refused to reward poor player behavior. His even-handedness when it came to the players was one of the reasons Penny loved him as a coach.

The referee placed the ball on the field between the two teams and raised his whistle to his lips. A horrendous boom behind Penny drowned out the referee and his whistle.

Everyone looked behind the bleachers in time to see a jagged fork of lightning split the boiling black clouds rushing in from the west. So much for the game beating the storm. Another crack of thunder pierced Penny's ears. Both the refs and the coaches started blowing their whistles and yelling for everybody to clear the fields.

Francine rolled her eyes. "And I skipped hot yoga for this."

"If you want to stay up in these aluminum stands and be electrocuted, fine!" Wila stood. "But get your scrawny ass out of my fu—" A third crack of thunder drowned the rest of her insult.

A blast of cold wind with even colder splatters of rain obviously spurred Francine more than Wila's insults. She jumped up and headed down the steps. Heaven forbid the weather ruined her perfectly highlighted blond coif.

Dani hung on to her coffee for dear life as she scrambled down as well. Penny followed, praying the clouds didn't cut loose before she reached the bottom. The last thing she needed was to slip on wet aluminum, tumble down the bleachers, and break her neck. She stepped onto the concrete, and heavier drops splashed on the slab that anchored the metal.

"Come on, Mom," Justine yelled. She took off for their vehicle, not pausing to make sure Penny followed, Dani's son Mark right behind her.

"Nice to know they're concerned about our welfare," Dani muttered.

Penny held up her keys and jangled them. "It's not like they can get in without us." They laughed and jogged after the kids.

"See you at girls' night!" Wila waved before heading in the direction of her painfully bright red ride with her son Derek.

Francine said nothing. She was too focused on grabbing Brittany and racing for their own vehicle.

Justine shrieked as the heavy drops turned into a deluge and yanked futilely at the back door latch. On the run herself, Penny hit the button on her key fob to unlock her minivan's doors. They were both soaked to the skin when they dove into the van.

"This just sucks!" Justine leaned over the center console to shout in Penny's ear. "Look at my hair! I spent an hour straightening it, and now, it's going to frizz!"

Penny rubbed her temples with her fingertips. The headache she'd chalked up to the incoming storm grew worse. "Please don't yell at me."

"I'm yelling because-because-b—" Justine jerked back. "Oh, my god! Get the door open! I'm gonna be—"

Penny's fingers couldn't move fast enough. Despite Justine's effort to turn aside, vomit shot all over the minivan's center console and the right sleeve of Penny's sweatshirt.

Including her unfinished pumpkin spice latte in the minivan's cup holder.

Acknowledgements

It's amazing to me that I've spent nearly eleven years as a writer. The ten-year mark is when I start to get bored with a career and look for my next challenge in life. But making up stories is the best thing I've ever done, and I have no intention of slowing down.

But I do not take this journey alone.

First of all much respect and admiration to Elaina Lee of For the Muse Design for her glorious covers and Jaye Manus for her stylish interiors. As I've said many times before, these ladies make me look good.

To my son Genius Kid whom I'm oh-so-proud of. GO ARMY!

To my Darling Husband who has been behind me every step of the way for the last twenty-seven and a half years. I love you!

And finally to my readers. Thanks for loving my stories. You folks are awesome!

Suzan Harden transitioned from writing information technology manuals for companies and legal articles for a law enforcement magazine to her first love, fantasy and science fiction in all their forms. She's the author of the Bloodlines, the 888-555-HERO, and the Justice series.

www.ingramcontent.com/pod-product-compliance
Lightning Source LLC
Chambersburg PA
CBHW070550100726

47907CB00004B/1326